About the Author

David Burt was evacuated from London to Yorkshire at the outbreak of WW2 and his education suffered accordingly. He started work on a building site at fifteen and a half and had a variety of job roles before becoming the CEO of a UK manufacturing company making components for Aerospace and electrical connectors for Formula 1 Race cars. During his career he was County Chairman for the CBI and on the Advisory Council for the BBC, before becoming the Chairman of the Regulatory Council for UK Optical services; he remains Chairman of the Consumer Complaints Service. He is a lifelong sculptor and has exhibited at the RA Summer Exhibition and he also rallies Classic Cars.

To Sonia Burt, my wife.
She has put up with my writing without complaint.

David Burt

SITUATIONS AND SURPRISES

AUSTIN MACAULEY
PUBLISHERS LTD.

A CIP catalogue record for this title is available from the British Library.

ISBN 9781786298508 (Paperback)
ISBN 9781786298515 (Hardback)
ISBN 9781786298522 (E-Book)

www.austinmacauley.com

First Published (2016)
Austin Macauley Publishers Ltd.
25 Canada Square
Canary Wharf
London
E14 5LQ

Contents

THE ANNUAL VILLAGE ART GROUP EXHIBITION

The evening gathering in the Village Hall was normally a relaxed and convivial affair for the forty or so regular painters of watercolour and oils in the Village Art Group.

Tonight however everyone was seated by their easels without a brush in action, as they talked in hushed undertones amongst themselves while they waited to find out if their paintings and photographs, worked on over the last twelve months, had been selected to be put on show in the Village Church during the week of the Harvest Festival celebrations.

Pam had just said, for about the third time to her good friend Peggy.

'I just feel worried about my painting.'

Peggy replied once again.

'Look, would you stop worrying, your painting is the best thing you have ever done. OK, it's different from the stuff you have been doing for years, and it challenges the viewer. Well that's what art is supposed to do. Even my photographs try to do that! People want to be challenged and stop to think about the issues of today, particularly right now over the immigration crisis in Europe and I'm sure your picture catches the mood.'

'I just wish my photographs for this year's show had anything like the bite of your painting.'

At this point Ms Cecilia Mason-Grant, known universally as Ms C.M hyphen G, President of the Art Group, swept into the hall leading the Vicar, the Reverend Phipson, and two members of the selection panel, both according to Peggy's views 'Ms C.M-G's stooges'.

It was rumoured that both ladies were associated as "artistic advisors" to an art shop and gallery in the local town, in which Ms C.M-G had a financial interest.

The President was wearing a large wide-brimmed hat in the autumn colour of rust, sporting what looked like a significant bunch of grapes on the band. She gripped the microphone and tapped it energetically to get attention, unnecessary in view of her hat!

In her most put on cultured voice the President addressed her flock.

'Friends and fellow artists, before I share this year's public exhibition selections with you I am delighted to confirm that Rev Phipson has been kind enough to agree the exhibition of our creative work will be shown in the Church as part of the Harvest Festival celebration, affording you all the opportunity to have your work seen by people from our village, other villages, the local media and well beyond.'

'Sounds like a commercial promotion for launching a new brand of soap flakes,' said Peggy to Pam out of the corner of her mouth.

'Now,' said Ms CM-G loftily, 'I am very pleased with the steady improvement in techniques so many of you have achieved this year and I intend to introduce some new innovations to our artistic and creative work next year.'

She paused, smiling in a self-satisfying way, as her eagle eye scanned the gathered amateur artists to make sure everyone was attentive to her pronouncements.

Most of the group could recall the last artistic initiative Ms C.M-G had introduced, an American Indian specialising in 'Body painting and Life sculpture' from Oklahoma, who it turned out was getting his teeth fixed for free on the NHS. Ms C.M-G had apparently engaged him after a conversation in the dentist's waiting room.

He was not a success!

'Finally,' said Ms C.M-G, with a look over at Rev Peabody who was by now glancing significantly at his watch.

'I have the committee's agreed list of pictures that will hang in the Church. One or two in both of our groups will sadly be disappointed this year as is the case every year, but for others I know this will be the spur to greater creative endeavour next year'.

‘Oh goodness,’ said Peggy to Pam in a cynical voice, ‘You would think she is the artistic leader of our group, not just the organiser.’

It was well known that Ms C.M-G’s Presidential role had developed over the years because of her love of organising village affairs. Her claimed degree in Art Appreciation was from a remote training establishment in Scunthorpe!

The group’s artistic supporter and technical help to any member was Hillary Butt, the local School Art Teacher, who was as ever sitting at the back of the hall and rarely received a mention from Ms C.M-G.

Ms C.M-G started calling out names of the photos to be exhibited and Peggy was pleased to hear her name and picture “Butterfly Nettles” being called.

Pam, who had for many years had one of her oil paintings in the annual exhibition, waited apprehensively as the President called the painters’ names. Her apprehension was based upon the painting she had chosen from her work based upon her response to the painful scenes, night after night, on television of immigrant people from Syria desperate to leave their country to avoid conflict and persecution and find a new life for themselves and their children in a safer country in Europe.

Pam had spent many hours drawing children’s hands and faces clawing their way through barbed wire before she had decided on the right balance to catch the drama and fear in her oil painting, and now standing there as the names of those to be shown were called, she knew the change from her traditional style of painting pastoral village scenes with village people was different and challenging.

The last painters' names were called and Ms C.M-G said briskly.

'Thank you all.'

Pam sighed and Peggy squeezed her hand and said in a choked voice.

'Never mind, your painting *is* good, scarily so, best you have ever done. The silly cow couldn't face up to hanging it so let's go and collect it together.'

Pam went up with Peggy and found her unframed picture easily enough and was just picking it up when Ms C.M-G bounced up, big hat and all.

'Oh, Pamela, we just felt your painting was a little too … well extreme for the exhibition this year. Now if you can go back to that nice style of yours with faces and people that we can all recognise as village people, I am sure we will find you a niche in our exhibition next year.' With this said, she swept on to dispense largess to the artists talking over their success or failures for the year.

On the way home when Pam had to pass Peggy's flat above the newspaper shop in the village square, Peggy said.

'Look, I have just had an idea. Would you mind letting me have your painting for a bit. I would love to spend a bit of time photographing it to catch the colour and mood of what you have done, and then you could send a copy or two out to your daughter in New Zealand. I know she would love that.'

'What a nice idea and you are right, I think Sally and the family would enjoy seeing the actual picture. I did share the ideas and my attempts to catch a mood with Sally on the phone whilst I was painting. Anyway I will have to think whether I need to go back to my old style.'

Peggy immediately said, 'You certainly should not go back to the 'folksy village people' scenes. You have to keep pushing the edges of your skill, as you have with your "Refugees at the border" painting.'

Peggy fitted Pam's large painting under one arm, holding the bottom edge with her fingers carefully.

'See you for coffee on Saturday. Bye for now,' she called over her shoulder as she made her way to her front door.

Life moved on steadily and without drama in the village, and the Church Harvest Festival added greatly to the villagers' social activity. The event itself added to Pam's workload as a Secretary in the nearby town Solicitor's office when the partners decided to invite several of their clients to a dinner in the best pub in the village with a visit to the Church exhibition, resplendent with autumn fruit, vegetables and flowers and the photographs and paintings on show.

The only drawback was that Pam had several times to explain to the partners, colleagues, even the lawyers' customers, that she was not showing a painting this year. She overcame this embarrassment by saying she was changing her style and was preparing for a bigger launch of her work the following year.

Initially Pam felt embarrassed by this fictitious story but it went down quite well and somehow helped with the pain she really felt by being overlooked.

Peggy met with Pam regularly for a coffee and mentioned she was enjoying practising her photographic techniques on Pam's oil painting.

They met as usual for a coffee and chat a week after the Harvest Festival show had finished and Peggy gave Pam several photographs of her painting which caught the colours and drama of her work perfectly.

Pam was delighted and declared her intention to send copies off to her daughter in Auckland, New Zealand the very next week.

Peggy then said to Pam.

'I'm so pleased you liked the shots, I thought them some of my best work. I am going to put one into a photographic competition in London. Would you mind if I kept the picture a bit longer in case the organisers want more shots?'

'Not at all,' said Pam, 'I hope you will be rather more successful than I was with the village exhibition.'

A month later over coffee Peggy said.

‘Guess what, I was successful with the photograph and have two tickets to the opening event in London. Would you mind supporting me?’

‘Love to,’ replied Pam and a few days later they made a trip to London.

Getting a cab from Victoria Station Pam found herself standing outside the entrance to the Royal Academy in the Strand.

‘Goodness, I had no idea you had been so successful, Peggy, in such a prestigious place, how marvellous.’

‘Well, I am a bit nervous now,’ said Peggy, ‘But here we go.’

Having shown her tickets at the entrance the two of them moved with the excited queue of exhibitors up the stairs and into the main foyer of the great building with Peggy holding firmly on to Pam’s arm.

‘We need Show Room 7,’ said Peggy, steering Pam steadily along amongst the crowd until the signs above the doors indicated the correct one.

Pam found herself shepherded into the room bursting with excited people standing in front of pictures of all sizes, subjects and shapes without a photograph being in sight.

Peggy stopped halfway down the room and Pam froze, on the wall in front of her was her oil painting with her name and title of the painting underneath.

Pam felt faint and completely confused as she gazed transfixed at her painting.

'Peggy, how on earth, what has happened?' Pam spluttered.

Peggy hugged Pam.

'Well, it is simple really. I knew your painting was good so I found out the entry procedure from the R.A. Summer Exhibition. I pretended to be you, sorry, and sent in one of my photos. I received the notification I was selected to bring up my painting to show the adjudicators, and incidentally one of a few hundred to be seen by them from the six thousand who sent in entries.

'I brought your painting up to the R.A. as they asked, on the Tuesday I told you I couldn't make coffee as I had to visit my aunt, and your "challenging" picture was selected. Congratulations.'

Pam was simply speechless with tears running down her cheeks.

'Well,' said Peggy, 'Now thousands of people are going to see your brilliant work. You are in the R.A. catalogue and you will find yourself in all sorts of Art journals as well as our local paper. Even high and mighty Ms C.M-G will have to wave her hat to you, like it or not! But much more important than that, now you have your own show and you have to keep developing your painting talents to make people think and to enjoy.'

THE PROPERTY MAN

'You have done WHAT!'

Lucy's voice hit an octave sufficiently high to cause the parrot to crouch, feathers puffed up, on her perch despite the fact that she was well used to high-pitched vocal renditions in the kitchen.

'I have bought 16 Creswell Street, a two-bedroom property in that nice Crescent of Victorian houses at the bottom of town.'

This message was delivered in measured tones by Ben, sufficiently normal for the parrot to disengage herself from her iron grip on the perch.

'Why, how, what for?' came a staccato stream of questions shot across the kitchen table.

When the one-sided interrogation had finally run out of breath, Ben said, 'Since I was laid off I have done nothing and had nothing worthwhile to do. Your life is busy with the house, the food, the garden, the Women's Institute, your keep fit, badminton. I'm in your 'territory' all the time.

‘I bought the house at auction using the money from my ISA, which was not producing any interest worth bothering about, and there is enough of the money for me to get the place tidied up before I sell it and hopefully keep myself active for a time and make a return on the capital.’

‘You weren’t laid-off, you retired on a pension,’ said Lucy, ‘In any case what do you know about building, you spent twenty-five years as a window cleaner and don’t tell me you are going to do all the work yourself. You are always grumbling about your knee and look at your “motor,” you must have put on a stone since you retired.’

Ben defensively drew in his stomach, unsuccessfully.

‘Well all the more reason for me to do something active,’ he said, ‘Anyway I have the keys and I am going to go into Number 16 tomorrow to decide what needs to be done.’

‘Look Ben,’ said Lucy in a rather more subdued tone, ‘Perhaps I haven’t noticed properly you were a bit fed-up. I am sorry and I expect when I get used to the idea I will be quite pleased you have found a challenge, but right now I am thinking of the trouble I have getting you to change a light bulb, let alone do anything technical around the house. Look, I will talk to Betty at the WI. Her husband has a building company, I am sure I can get her to help.’

‘No you won’t.’

Ben said this with such vigour that the parrot, who had been busily pecking its corn on the cob, squawked back on a seed and retreated into its feathers on its perch.

'I am going to see this project through in my way on my own, thank you.'

This said, Ben picked up the Daily Mail from the table and swept out of the kitchen, leaving Lucy staring at her half empty cup of tea in considerable surprise.

'Well, in forty years,' she muttered to herself before dialling her daughter in Leeds who made her mother recount the events twice before she believed it, despite the fact that she was being badgered by her children to get them to school.

'Look, Mum, just leave him alone to do it. I am sure you could get some of your contacts to sort things out properly but it is his money and when it flops it will be easier for you to manage him. Let's face, it he couldn't sort out William's Meccano when he was trying to build a windmill, remember? There is no chance he can renovate this house.'

It has to be said that Ben had the same thing on his mind as he approached the front door of his new property with a large writing pad and pen. Two hours later he had filled two foolscap pages with activities he thought needed at least looking at, if not repairing or replacing.

Sitting somewhat disconsolate in the Takeaway Tea Shop over a cup of tea and a mince tart, supplied free by the proprietor whose comment, 'Least I could do after all the years you've cleaned my shop front so well.'

Ben put down beside each Action item on his property list the name of a local contractor who might be able to help him sort out the fairly dilapidated and rather care worn condition of Number 16.

Deciding the electrics in the property should be checked for safety, Ben walked down the High Street to Buckland Electrical Suppliers and Contractors. This business was an old cleaning contract of his and he therefore went behind the shop counter to the owner's office as he had done for twenty-five years to have a cup of tea, or something stronger at Christmas and special events, after he had finished cleaning the considerable shop front windows each week.

'Ben, nice to see you. Have you come back to do the windows?' said Mr Buckland as he swung out of his swivel chair and shook Ben's hand, 'They have not been done properly since you retired.'

'Laid off,' corrected Ben, 'Actually I need a bit of advice.' He then proceeded to give Mr Buckland all the detail of his new venture.

Mr Buckland's response was to get his coat and walk down to 16 Creswell Street with Ben to look around.

At the end of an hour's inspection Mr Buckland said.

'Look, I would like a good young apprentice I have to check out all the wiring. I suspect we should bring the fuse board up to current speck and I can see the need for six or eight new wall plugs. Otherwise things don't look in too bad a condition.'

'Is this going to cost me much?' enquired Ben, 'I'm trying to cover things with a bit of a limited budget.'

'Look,' replied Mr Buckland, 'You did a great job for me, what twenty-five years ago? I will get everything checked at our cost. Good experience for the apprentice. If I have to send anyone to put in new plugs, etc., I will just charge you for the components. Fair enough?'

Over the next three weeks, plumbers, decorators, window frame replacements were all tackled by his old client group who specialised in the specific techniques. Happy without any real encouragement or inducement from Ben to "thank him" for his years of attention, keeping their shop windows in sparkling condition week after week, year after year. Most with the comment that if he picked up the trade again, he would be immediately engaged.

Ben kept progress "out of sight" from Lucy, knowing she was expecting him to ask her for help to get him out his difficulty by getting one of her many contacts to clear up one mess or another.

Ben meantime laboured cheerfully clearing up before and after each contractor, dumping the residue into a hired skip parked in Cresswell Street that was donated by the Skip Hire Company, another of his long-standing customers.

Over three months Ben was able to stand to one side in the bathroom and see his "motor" had significantly diminished a reduction that gave reason for the several pounds difference in his rating on the bathroom scales.

Lucy who had shared Ben's redundancy and risky step into the unknown with several close girlfriends as well as her daughter, had to admit that Ben was a good deal less irritable about the place in the evenings now that he spent almost every day at Number 16.

Finally, Lucy said, 'Why cannot I come down to see the place now you are close to finishing?' and was pleased to hear Ben say.

'Of course what about tomorrow on your way back from badminton?'

After going around Number 16 in silence, Lucy said.

'It's really very nice. Any young couple would be pleased to live here.'

'Well,' said Ben, 'I certainly hope so as its going into the auction next week and the agent seems to think the price range will give me a handsome turn on my investment. Perhaps a thirty percent gain in under six months.'

Lucy felt some of her previous comments might have been a little harsh and indicated this to Ben with, 'I don't know how you have managed it, but you really have.'

As she stood there Lucy continued to let her mind run through various thoughts as to the future.

'We will be able to change my little motor for something more up to date. It's about time I knocked the smile off Sheila after that banker husband of hers bought her that BMW and I can finally go to Canada and spend a bit of time with my sister. I'm quite sure Ben won't want to make that trip.'

Ben had seen several young couples who had visited Number 16. The majority saying, 'What a great first house it would make for them but getting a mortgage to cover the Agents estimate of what the house was likely to get at auction was going to be beyond their range.'

Ben quickly realised that Number 16 was likely to go to a retired couple 'downsizing' as the Agent put it and well able to make the purchase.

Looking back to the days when Ben had scrabbled at the time of his marriage to find the deposit necessary to get a mortgage on the modest little two bedroomed flat and remembered that without help from his, by no means wealthy parents, he and Lucy would never have got started on the property ladder, Ben felt sad as he recalled the sadness of several young couples who had seen Number 16 as a step beyond them.

The auction, offering a range of properties, including Number 16, was very well attended and Ben was able to explain to Lucy how his property had exceeded the Agents' and his own expectations by several thousand pounds.

Lucy positively beamed and thoughts of selecting her new car and fixing her flights dominated her thinking as Ben said.

'And making sure I keep busy, I bid for and bought the old youth hostel building in the Market Square and have made enough to refit it as flats for young couples wanting to get on to the property ladder.'

'You have done WHAT!' exploded a shocked Lucy as the parrot shrank into her ruffled feathers.

WEEKLY INFORMER

Lucy sat down on the seat against the wall in the airport under the huge "Arrivals" sign where she decided she could read her briefing file before her appointment with the Security Duty Officer.

Opening the thin folder headed "Lucy Foster, Reporter Weekly Informer Strictly Private," she looked through the few paragraphs which identified her required role during the morning.

"Assess and report on the Airport Security Management of the incoming passenger flow through Security, taking note of any 'bottleneck' that might be caused by the recent reduction in staffing levels or process treatment of specific incoming passenger groups. Read the report written on these subjects twelve months ago and comment in your Report on any clear cases describing deterioration or service improvements.

"During your investigations under no circumstances indicate your interest to any passenger within the Security area, or respond should a passenger or passengers approach you. As a Press representative you are required to wear your *Weekly Informer* Reporter's badge."

Lucy looked through a pink copy of an unnamed reporter's article dated almost exactly a year earlier. The report was heavy with the statistical details of the numbers of passengers passing through the various Security checkpoints to get their Passport clearance and entry into the country.

The only comments by the reporter were personal observations on frustration and stress when passengers, not speaking English, were shepherded through the automated passport unit designed to speed up the process by bye-passing the personal passport investigation by the Airport's security operators.

Hardly a word, Lucy noted, in the article which indicated anything of the colour and national variations in the hordes of people arriving into the country.

"Horribly impersonal, all statistics and boredom and now I have to write the same sort of uninteresting 'no one will read' article myself, how boring," Lucy thought, "That pompous sub-editor never wanted a girl reporter on his bloody paper and he takes that out on me." Lucy sat fuming. "That mean-minded old fool sending me to report on three funeral events for local dignitaries, then sent me to report on that Finance and General Purposes Council Committee all day meeting, making sure I missed out on the Pageant through the town and the local flower show.

“I hate this job … well, I don’t hate the job but I do hate the boring stuff I get sent to report on. Oh crikey what’s the time? I cannot be late for my appointment.”

Hurriedly gathering her things together, Lucy went to the “Staff Entrance Only” door and pushed the entry button. She approached the middle-aged, rather rotund and balding Security Sergeant seated comfortably behind the high desk who smiled at her arrival and said, ‘Now you have to be the Ace Reporter from the *Weekly Informer*,’ and glancing at his screen he said, ‘Lucy Foster? Could I see your authorisation paper please?’ holding out an oversized hand, ‘We have to be so careful with our procedures nowadays.’

“That’s OK,” said Lucy, holding out her Press Pass and her *Weekly Informer* authorisation for the Airport event.

‘Sergeant,’ said Lucy, leaning her head at an acute angle to read his badge, ‘Your badge is upside down so I cannot establish if you are the Security Chief or an Australian.’

Sergeant Lipten roared with laughter as he rotated his badge. ‘Thank goodness’, he finally said, ‘You spotted that. My boss would have had me demoted on the spot if he had caught me. Well, young lady, I am delighted to give you this Security Pass that will let you move anywhere within the Airport Security area, except the interview rooms.’

Sergeant Lipten became conspiratorial as he said, ‘You probably know, Lucy, the Airport management are very jumpy about letting you report on managing passenger arrivals, and they only agreed because the Airport Management Board insisted due to the fact, as I recall, the young man from your paper made a pretty boring job of the article last year.'

'If it helps, Lucy', continued the Sergeant, 'Here is last week's stats sheet on throughput in each section. I shouldn't really let you have it but you've saved me being stuffed, so I owe you, and this should save you some counting time. Don't tell any of the Security Officers in there you have just blackmailed me into giving you the data, or I will be in more trouble. Good luck.'

Lucy passed from the inner sanctum of Airport Security into the maelstrom of the passport and Security Department for all arriving passengers. With the Security and Reporters' badges predominantly placed, she edged her way to a point where she could see all eight booths with their individual Security Operator, each with a line of arrivals and a corralled zig zag queue of some two hundred people waiting to join the next nearly available officer, directed by several yellow coated Security Operators who were constantly beckoning and pointing at the patiently waiting passengers.

Lucy sighed, as she recalled she was here to observe the people processing times, and she scribbled notes before she concentrated upon the travellers offering their faces and passports for automatic clearance.

Lucy also noted the way the Security people were playing their role to help individuals, and frequently their families, through the theoretically simple automated procedures, assisting the never-ending flow of passengers.

An hour later back in the airport public area to have a coffee and gather her thoughts, Lucy decided the throughput of passengers was significantly better than her colleague had noted a year earlier. Therefore, the management were doing a better job.

This considered, Lucy felt her professional capabilities as a reporter were being challenged if she was forced to follow the statistically based views taken by her colleague without reflecting something of the colour and interest of the steady flow of people from many corners of the world making their way through Arrival Security.

Sitting back in the same seat on which she had started her morning, Lucy watched the flow before her. The row of waiting car drivers standing solemnly in their dark suits with large cards held across their chest, identifying the name of the arrival passenger to be transported in comfort somewhere into the country.

Lucy decided the line looked rather like criminals with their nameplates solemnly waiting to go to the Tower of London! The sombre line making a backdrop to the joyous children, husband, wife, grandparents, waiting with flowers and flags to cheer, embrace and hug their arriving relatives, often in a happy flow of tears and photographs.

Whereas the seasoned travellers with their earphones and wheeled luggage were steadily wending their way through the holiday groups, all following their tour guides' raised banners.

Lucy became emotionally dazzled by the scene in front of her without any idea of how to encapsulate some of the colour as she struggled to think of a "hat peg" idea on which to hang her article on.

Suddenly Lucy realised in all the flowing human tide passing in front of her seat there was a small stationary figure who she had noted for some time without registering, an elderly black man, not a great deal taller than his upright suitcase, standing as if frozen in time under the information board whilst passengers swept by on either side.

Viewing him from her seat, Lucy realised he was looking neither to the right nor to the left, he was simply waiting.

Several minutes later Lucy was no farther forward finding some excitement and colour to make her article on Security Management less bland and was thinking she better get back to the office to write the article when she realised the old gentleman had still not moved or adjusted his stance since she had first spotted him.

Lucy then realised she could not possibly leave the Airport without at least asking if the old boy needed any help.

Making sure her Press and Security badges were clear, she made her way through the crowd and stood in front of the elderly gentleman, who was certainly no taller than she was.

'Are you alright, Sir, is someone picking you up,' Lucy enquired.

The response was careful and measured 'I am from St Lucia,' said the gentleman, without further comment.

'Yes, but is somebody coming to collect you?' she persisted.

'My daughter, come … maybe!' he replied.

'Why don't you come over to the seats just there and wait for your daughter,' said Lucy as she realised the old gentleman was very tired and confused by the passing flow of people, and without further ado Lucy took the handle of his rather battered suitcase and beckoned him to follow as she went back to a seat.

They both sat down, 'Now your daughter can see you here. What is her name?' asked Lucy slowly.

He let out a sigh, 'Don't know, she married.'

Lucy's reporting background was beginning to kick in as the old gentleman was giving her hints.

'What is your daughter's first name?' Lucy asked, again slowly.

'MARISHA,' he replied, 'She live in London town, now she married. Don't know name.'

‘I work here’, exaggerated Lucy, pointing at her badges, ‘so perhaps I can help. Do you have a mobile telephone?’ and she put her own phone to her ear in demonstration.

‘No phone,’ was the reply.

‘No, oh well have you got an address if you are going to London Town.’ Lucy asked, keeping her voice calm.

The old gentleman fumbled in his pocket and produced a slip of paper that simply said, “Croydon, London, England.”

Lucy felt she was getting nowhere and so she tried another tack exclaiming, ‘My name is Lucy. What’s your name?’ and received the reply.

“DALE.”

Hoping to maintain the one-sided conversation she asked, ‘Dale, what does your daughter do in Croydon?’

She was quite surprised when his extensive reply was, ‘She good for St Lucia plant and flower in Croydon, England.’

This had to be important and Lucy decided his daughter must be selling the many exotic plants found in St Lucia in Croydon.

Further discussion provided no more information on an address or telephone number, although it did establish Dale had been standing there waiting for over three hours for his daughter to appear and he was clearly very happy that Lucy was offering some help.

Lucy decided in order to be of help she had to think like a reporter and she phoned her friend, a colleague in the *Weekly Informer* office – Beryl.

'Bee, I have a funny one here at the airport. Please could you go on line and get the number of any Croydon florist selling plants and flowers from St Lucia in the West Indies.'

Ten minutes later Bee was back with three florist numbers that might sell exotic plants.

Lucy phoned two flower shops and asked if she could talk to Marisha without a response but the third call had a Marisha on the line.

Lucy said, 'I am at the Airport and talking to Dale who I understand is your father?'

'Oh, mother of God, he is supposed to be flying from St Lucia tomorrow. Is he alright? Oh my, I must shut up the shop and get the children from school,' said Marisha in a panicky voice.

Lucy said, 'Just a minute. I am a reporter working here at the airport this morning. I may be able to help to get your Dad to you. Give me your shop address. OK, now I will call you back in ten minutes. Do nothing until I do, your Dad's a lovely man and he is quite safe.'

Lucy made sure Dale would stay where she had seated him whilst she put back on the Security Badge and went into the Security Office to smile at the

Sergeant. 'Goodness gracious, I thought you had gone back to the paper to do your article', he exclaimed.

'Well I had intended to', said Lucy, 'But then I saw this elderly West Indian gentleman, marooned in the reception area' and she recounted the whole story with the request. 'Now as I 'saved' you from being told off, could you help me get the old boy to his daughter's shop in Croydon?'

'Course I can. We regularly have to help lost and strays get home from the airport,' and he picked up his phone and spoke for a few minutes. 'OK, now go back and sit with the old gentleman, a police officer will there in a minute and take over. OK now, are honours even?'

'Honours even,' Lucy replied, 'I will phone his daughter the good news and thanks a million. Read my article in next week's paper. I bet you notice a mention of "a special security officer" and his excellent service.'

Lucy had an unexpected text from her pompous sub-editor a week later.

'Lucy, the editor was impressed with your interesting and colourful article on the airport security and the way you introduced the personal touch. We would like you to do an article for the paper this week on the Queen Victoria Hospital, Emergency Services.'

GOING OUT OF BUSINESS

'I know it's very difficult for you to accept, Andy, but the last two year's financial facts are on the paper in front of you and as you know from the bank's letter, they are now insisting something is done "to repay your overdraft" otherwise you will be out of business.'

This said, Harold put the letter down on his impressive desk next to the label on the desk announcing to every client that he was "Harold Pearson, Accountant."

Andy stared dumbly over his Accountant's head at the large wall clock clicking loudly and ominously over Harold's seat as he removed his handkerchief from his pocket and dabbed his forehead to wipe away the perspiration. It wasn't just the broken sleep that made him feel so feverish, it was the effect of weeks of worry that had seen matters decline in the company until the arrival of the bank's final demand letter.

Although by no means a sensitive man, Harold became concerned by the signs of stress as his client dabbed his forehead. He picked up one of the three telephones on his desk which was immediately answered.

'Jane would you bring in two teas for me please, Mr Walters does take sugar, and perhaps a few biscuits.'

Harold put the phone down gently and turned to Andy, 'Now, Andy, let's just run through the position to see if we are missing something.'

Andy nodded slowly.

'Now let's see,' continued Harold, looking at his considerable file of papers for Walters Engineering Ltd. After you lost the A.M. Motors contract to the … who was it? Oh right, those Chinese suppliers, you have been unable to fill,' and here Harold glanced at his file summary, 'fifty per cent of your machining capacity?'

Andy nodded, without comment.

'You said when we last met that more of your old customers are turning to China,' and again Harold looked at the file as he went on, 'or India to get their components machined, and try as you might you just cannot compete with the prices being offered? The position, you said, is that the service you have built up for over twenty years in the business has been based upon quality and the machined metal work finish that you offered but these standards for volume components are no longer considered worth paying a premium for, if the Asian components are adequate for the job and the supply for volume items is reliably maintained?'

Harold looked up as Jane came into the office with the tea tray.

'Now have some tea and tell me is this still the position?'

The question was couched rather more to get Andy out of his state of depressed silence than to expect a response, the question he already knew the answer to!

'Yes,' said Andy, 'And I am fairly sure that another customer with an annual contract coming up for review next month will go with a Chinese supplier and that will represent another five or six percent of my present workload.'

'OK,' said Harold, sipping his tea, 'Now the remaining, say, forty or so percent of the order book is … I think you said "short batch work". I think you also said it was generally required in lots of a few hundred rather than thousands of parts, and these clients need top quality as well as totally reliable delivery?'

Andy nodded his head in agreement.

'Right', said Harold, 'It is clear if the business is not to be declared bankrupt and the bank at the end of this month force a sale of all your machines to get their overdraft back, you will need to think about selectively selling off several of your CNC Mills, etc., that are not working, and I'm sorry to say, let several of your people go.'

Andy looked at the clock and blew his nose, 'I know it's me managing the cutback or the bank doing it their way, but I just don't know how I can face making three, perhaps four, people redundant just to suit the bloody bank,' said Andy miserably.

'You know I have brought up a great team over the last twenty years, most of them from school or apprenticeships. What are they going to do here in the village? Nothing, go on the dole, there is not another machine shop within thirty miles and none that I know of at that distance are doing well enough to take on extra staff.'

Andy continued thinking out loud. 'You know, Harold, I have put every penny I had saved up, including my pension fund, into trying to keep going over the last two years and here is the bank demanding twenty-five grand payback on the overdraft they were happy to lend three years ago. My efforts just haven't worked.'

Harold came round the desk and sat in the seat next to Andy.

'Well, look, Andy, it must be better to keep a few of your people and machines working rather than letting the bank collapse the whole company? I am sure your CNC machines will get a good sale price, you have always gone for the best, and even I can see you keep the machines and the workshop in immaculate condition. So once you have gone through the necessary laying-off some of the workforce, you can continue to run the company for the short-batch precision customers and I wouldn't be surprised if you couldn't section off a half of the building and offer it to a storage company and get a bit of rental income that way.'

By seven o'clock the next morning Andy had gathered himself together, unshaven, but sitting in his office off the shop floor. He had made a list of as many of the unpleasant things he would have to do to pay off the bank and hopefully keep some remnants of his company together. He went to his office door, taking in the sweet smell of the working machines and relishing the tidy discipline of the shop in front of him, trying not to let the terrible feelings overcome him that very soon much of the scene would be no better than a 'rump' of his company.

Andy waved at his shop floor supervisor and beckoned him over to the office.

Fred Jones, immaculate in his company overalls as always, walked between the CNC machines looking left and right checking for any sign of machine, or operator problems. It was said on the shop floor that Fred could sense, from his supervisor's booth, if a spindle speed was not at the operational level required for the job on a machine.

Fred came into the office and Andy waved him into the seat opposite him.

'Well, I have gone through everything with the accountant and nothing has changed from when I showed you the bank letter. We really have a week to save what we can and show the bloody bank we will be able to pay off the overdraft and then sort out how we can keep going. If I can't raise enough to pay off the overdraft, or take too long, the bank will declare us bankrupt. I just want you to know if everything fails, Hammersley Engineering would love you in their team and I'm sure they would pay better than I do, which would be some compensation for the couple of hours extra travel.'

Fred cut in.

'Look, Andy, I'm not a kid anymore. I am going to see this out with you, so go on with your, "Whatever we have left" after we have sorted the bank. OK?'

Andy looked at Fred, 'Thanks, Fred, needless to say I certainly need your support. I have just spoken to a machine agent on the phone who happens to be the main man at Willoughbys and he is coming down Wednesday next week with his people. You will remember he came round a year or so ago when he said he is certain he can place the list of machines I gave him at top dollar, which should be enough with a cutback in the salary bill for the bank to recognise they will get their money, even if it takes a few months. I agree your list of the guys who we will have to let go, and I have factored in statutory redundancy rates plus two; best we can do for the guys.'

Andy blew his nose vigorously.

Fred stood up, 'OK, best get back to the machines,' he said. 'By the way you won't forget you promised that nice lady Vicar, Angela, that you would support the 'Village Day' she has organised for this Saturday so that people can walk round the village and get a feel of the place. You know, the church, the garden centre, the car repair place. Almost everyone has opened up to the event.'

'Oh great, can't we get out of it now? Just what we needed,' exclaimed Andy.

'Well, I don't think so,' said Fred, 'And I don't think we should. I have two of the apprentices sorted to guide the people around and we will only run two machines as a demonstration and the lads are coming in, unpaid, and everyone has got everything up spotless for Saturday, which must help when the machine agents come round next week. You don't have to do anything and the village will appreciate the effort.'

'Sorry,' said Andy, 'You are quite right. I will be here anyway getting the machine specs together for next week. Go ahead as you planned.'

Saturday was at its autumnal best and people in the village turned out in droves to support the day, organised to encourage village togetherness as a community.

In his office with his table covered in machine specifications, Andy could hear the subdued hubbub of people talking as they moved between the yellow lines and stood looking at the high-speed computer aided turning machines at work.

Towards the end of the afternoon, Fred tapped on the door with a mug of tea.

'Everything has gone very well. People really appreciated you opening the place up. There is a gentleman who has been here for an hour or so and clearly knows something about manufacturing technology. I had a chat with him and he asked if he could shake your hand. I did say you were very busy but he seems very anxious to see you.'

'OK,' said Andy, 'I could do with a break for a few minutes. Wheel him in.'

Fred came back a few minutes later with a distinguished looking middle-aged gentleman, sporting a blazer and a silk handkerchief in his top pocket and as Fred retreated the gentleman introduced himself.

'James Beacham,' he said as he proffered his card that gave the appropriate information, "James Beacham, MBE, CEO, St&S UK Ltd." 'The ST&S stands for Sailing Technology and Supplies, a bit of a mouthful. Please call me James. May I sit down? I won't take much of your time.'

'Of course,' said Andy, clearing some of his papers from the seat, 'My name is Andy. I'm sorry there are papers everywhere but I am planning a reorganisation,' he said rather ruefully.

'Well,' said James, 'May I complement you and your team, this machine shop is the best I have seen and in my business I have visited many here and abroad over the years. Your Supervisor, Fred, was most informative and this is really why I asked to see you as you might be able to help me.'

Andy laughed, 'Well I'm afraid we don't do anything for the sailing profession, it's more car parts and components we cover here.'

'No, I understand that, but I have a problem. I should explain,' said James, 'I have only just moved to the village with my family. I bought the Manor House and I am trying to bring my design people into the stables when I can convert them into office units.'

'I congratulate you,' said Andy, 'I know your beautiful house quite well as I have been there once or twice with the last owners. You are a lucky man.'

'Well yes, but for the business I have a real problem which is why I decided to take the Village Day walk to try to clear my mind,' replied James.

'My business has supplied sailing gear and technology quite successfully over the last twenty years but if I can be very open with you, Andy, I have just hit a rock.'

'I know the feeling,' said Andy, rather bitterly.

James continued, 'One of my biggest customers runs the America's Cup Competition, a world-wide event, I'm sure you have heard of the races?'

'Of course,' said Andy, 'Yacht racing by huge sailing boats half way around the world.'

'That's right' James went on, 'The sponsors put millions of dollars into all the several categories of yachts by size which races under the America's Cup rules and from next year they are introducing global surveillance cameras on every yacht so that as organisers they can oversee sailing procedures and TV companies will get live pictures by satellite links throughout all the races. I have been contracted to put the package together.'

'Good grief,' said Andy, 'Well done. It sounds like a huge job.'

'It is,' said James, 'And we have all the contracts in place for cameras, sensors, etc., but I am in real trouble over the stainless steel brackets, bulkhead fittings and all the prescribed metal work necessary to bolt the electronic gear in place and keep it there, whatever the weather.

'Looking at your equipment and getting background from Fred, I have no doubt you could do the job if you would consider taking it on, even though I am well behind schedule at this point.'

'Yes, but–' interjected Andy.

'No please let me finish the picture, Andy, before you consider matters,' James hurried on, 'I have all the component drawings but my people are stuck until I can move them into the offices at the Manor, so I cannot start to look for suitable high quality suppliers.

'Fred gave me to believe if he and your team had the drawings as I described then they could convert programmes on your computer-aided machines quite quickly. I would be so grateful if you could give me priority on printing the first twenty sets. I would pay you up front thirty grand just to give me the next six months to sort out my offices and people. Fred said that could be a very useful sum just now.'

Andy's mouth was open but no sounds came out.

'And then I would give you a two-year contract to supply us all the precision metal parts, at your price, if you would take on the job to get me out of my problem.' James finished, looking expectantly at Andy.

Andy closed his mouth.

'Well,' he said, 'You came in at the nick of time.'

This said he took the long list he had drawn up under the heading 'Meeting Next Week' listing Machine Sales – Values, Redundancy – Individuals, and with a smile on his face Andy slowly and deliberately tore the sheet of paper into small pieces.

'Well there goes my reorganisation,' he said, 'Now let's get down to how my company can help you over your problems…'

'SOUTHERN RAIL ARE SORRY TO ANNOUNCE A DELAY'

The car park was very nearly full with a space at the bottom of the hill, the farthest it was possible to be from the ticket machine.

Getting into the space and out into the rain did nothing to calm Cliff Rogers stress levels. He pulled his coat collar up as he trudged to the coin machine, relieved to find he had the five pounds in coins necessary to avoid the excessive fine threat promoted in large letters on the daily and weekly charges notice board.

Gathering his ticket, he noted on the back the promotion of an optical services company.

'They need glasses to spot empty spaces,' thought Cliff wryly.

On trudging back to his car, en-route he was accosted by a man also wrapped in his raincoat, enquiring if he knew where the ticket machine was.

Cliff explained and with an apology the driver asked, 'As you know this place and I have never been before, could you direct me to the railway station as it seems to be quite divorced from its own car park.'

'You are right,' said Cliff, 'Look, I have time before my London train, get your car park ticket and I will wait here under this bit of cover and show you the route as it is a little complicated, particularly in this dreadful weather.'

The two men joined up and made their way across a narrow footbridge over the railway lines to the station entrance where both bought day return tickets to Victoria station, and a dubious cup of coffee from a machine proclaiming "every style of coffee drink at the push of a button."

Standing with their plastic coffee cups, waiting for the 10.37 train to arrive and happy to be under cover from the teaming rain, they exchanged names. Henry Paul introduced himself with thanks for the assistance and Cliff responded with Cliff Rogers and said 'I'm a Complaints Adviser for a company supplying products to help older people get by. I'm off to London for a meeting with my boss.'

Henry explained that his day had started at breakfast for a local meeting and he also had to meet with his boss for a lunch review and had unfortunately to visit the head office in London to do so. He went on to explain that he was responsible for promoting financial services to ex-service men and women.

Their "get to know you" discussions were interrupted by the station announcer declaring 'Southern

Rail are sorry to announce a delay to their ten-thirty-seven service owing to a line failure at Clapham. There will be a further announcement in fifteen minutes.'

'Oh, hell,' said Henry, 'My boss gets really wound up if anyone is late'.

'Well I hope this delay is not going to hold me up either,' replied Cliff, 'As I have a meeting to explain why some of the training of company personnel has not gone too well. If I don't get to the meeting at the start I worry that my assistant, who is not very experienced and inclined to talk too much when he is anxious, will say far too much to the boss and that could easily make a difficult situation a whole lot worse'.

Figuratively arm-in-arm in anxiety, the discussion followed an exchange of business cards and more shared concerns as the minutes ticked by.

Finally, the 10.37 train, now transformed into the 11.00 o'clock Southern service arrived and Cliff and Henry found seats opposite each other for the train's numerous stops to Victoria Station.

The discussion turned in a companionable way to the activities that Cliff and Henry were going to be engaged in whilst in London, and in the convivial way that rail travel hardships encourage, both felt more relaxed than they normally would to share their worries and concerns.

No time was taken up exchanging an inflated view of success and status, designed to puff up the ego, a regular enough routine in travel to London that the listening business person rarely believes but on the other hand cannot completely discard, just in case there is an element of truth which they might be able to utilise or manipulate to his or her advantage.

There is something about a stop-start train trip which dulls resolve and fairly soon Henry was explaining, in detail, his disappointment and feeling of lost integrity as the demands of his investment banking advisory role had squeezed out his former attitude to rules of conduct that ten years as an officer in the army had developed and encouraged.

'Now' Henry explained to Cliff, 'I am expected to use my military connections. Because of my army job I have details of several hundred men and women able, and damaged in conflict, on my records, many of whom I know personally. Now I am expected to tout for and promote our financial service investment programmes, irrespective of any doubts or concerns I might have based upon my understanding of the financial position of the ex-service personnel and then press them to take the product.'

'Sometimes,' Henry admitted, shamefacedly, 'When the individual clearly is relying on my words as an ex-officer to make their own decision. I'm really beginning to dislike what I see in the mirror every morning when I shave but what do I do? I have a daughter at University and with my mortgage and the normal cost of living, my ten year military pension would not go very far to cover all that, and in any case if I lose this job I am more than likely to wind up as a delivery driver.'

Henry sat back after this expose looking decidedly dejected.

Ignoring the rest of the passengers in the carriage, all buried in their papers or iPads, the two continued their review in undertones. Cliff responded to Henry's revelations with sympathy based upon his own experiences and his call to the head office meeting that day.

Partly instinctively to offer some sort of comfort to Henry as one stressed professional to another, Cliff quickly found himself unburdening his own problems to a willing listener.

'I am fed up trying to manage consumer complaints, training to people in the group who couldn't care less what the customer wants and are really only motivated by the size of their bonus when they exceed their sales targets, and since the products are all directed, theoretically, to help retired people who are often rather gullible when thinking through what might be an assistance to them as their vigour, eyesight, hearing, etc., declines, there is a constant stream of complaint about overselling and pressure sales for unnecessary products.'

Cliff continued to talk as he felt he was putting into words the frustration he was feeling.

'Despite these problems growing and the group marketing assurance that our customer integrity code comes first, I find the endless unlisted training lessons and schemes more and more disheartening and I am fairly sure I am going to get another lecture from my boss about helping to reduce the complaints statistics without having any hope of getting the help or support I would need to do so, despite the fact that I have a background in administration and experience to put things right.'

There was the warmth of shared experiences as they shook hands on arriving at Victoria Station and wished each other well at the ticket barrier before they each took their individual route into the Underground passageways which sucked them, with thousands of others, into their journey to their respective destinations under the streets of London.

The day moved on and both men met their professional tormentors as bravely as circumstances and their status allowed before wearily they left their individual offices, greatly relieved to be on the way back to Victoria for the return train journey home.

'Southern Rail are sorry to announce delays to the following trains owing to a derailment at Clapham Junction,' was the announcement that met Cliff as he stood with hundreds of other potential commuters staring up at the electronic board flashing change after change.

'The 4.05 to Lewes has been delayed.'

'The 4.20 to Lewes has been cancelled.'

On and on the bad news was flashed up.

'What a perfectly awful day,' thought Cliff sinking further into a feeling of despair!

‘I thought that was you,’ Henry said as he came up to Cliff’s shoulder in the crush. ‘Look, I’ve been here for half an hour and I have spoken to the assistant supervisor who happens to be an ex-serviceman I know. He tells me there is no hope they will get the broken down train at Clapham going for another hour and has given me the details of a local café he knows, called his mate who runs it just round the corner in Victoria Street and suggests we go round there. Come on let’s get a cup of tea out of this scrum!’

Seated with a chintzy tablecloth, a large pot of tea plus a couple of scones “on the house” delivered by the proprietor, ex-Sergeant Rogers, Cliff felt immensely better.

‘How did your day go, Henry?’ he said turning to him.

‘Crap, absolute crap. I got read the riot act for not pushing more products through my network. They know my service and field role engages with many more, now ex-service men and women than I have admitted to, and now they are insisting I give them the full list so they can unleash more of their sales dogs, who of course have not actual service experience. I refused and just walked out of the office. Of course, it’s the end of the road for me and I will have to start looking for some sort of paid employment tomorrow but somehow I feel relieved.’

‘Well done and bravely so,’ said Cliff, ‘Look, I have been thinking while you were talking. I should be a good deal gutsier about my miserable situation. I left my manager saying I would try to get better results when I know it's not possible, and I have to 'bite the bullet' and tell them to 'stuff their job'. Now I'm sitting here I am beginning to think about your network of ex-service men and women and their range of skills, most of them needing to occupy their time, earn some supplementary income to enhance their pension, able and disabled ex-Service people. Clearly there is no better time than now to move on and properly use my years of administrative management. What do you think – is there any way we could put our skills and experience together?'

'Wait a minute you mean we could build a cooperative company helping ex-service personnel get part-time employment, if not full time, to provide a service to householders using all the skills in which these service people have been trained?' said Henry as he stirred his second cup of tea.

'Well now as I think about it. I'm always being asked to suggest an ex-service person who might help in the short term, you know, like looking after a property whilst the family are on holiday, fill in when staff are on holiday, vehicle maintenance jobs, or security roles, when extra staff are needed for agricultural shows, that sort of thing!'

Walking back to Victoria Station, the 6.05 was waiting on platform 18 as it should be, and the two men continued their animated discussion as they settled into their seats to continue their journey towards a new company.

THE SUPERVISOR

'Geraldine, I do think sometimes you are a little hard on your girls.'

Geraldine let this oft-heard observation drift out of the open window of the HR Manager's spacious office.

In the silence that followed, Aubrey Livingstone's long fingers tapped hand to hand in an arch with his elbows on the arms of his swivel chair. His usual pose when he was anxious, as Geraldine knew well from several years of engagement on matters related to her management of the company's secretaries.

As usual Aubrey cracked first as he said.

'You see, we have to safeguard the caring culture we have built up with the staff and,' he hesitated, 'Just occasionally, Geraldine, well now and then, your actions with the girls give the impression of being a little, well how can I put this – heavy handed?' Aubrey trailed off apologetically.

Geraldine shifted slightly in her seat so that her well discussed long and slender legs showed themselves to a slightly better effect, causing Aubrey to focus upon her knees, as she knew he would, and as she expected his face took on a slightly pink hue.

Geraldine then launched forth.

'I don't think the MD or the Board would thank me if I allowed the company's secretaries team to take time out for every head cold or period pain.'

'No, no, of course not,' said Aubrey, 'And you run a very tidy ship. Everyone knows that and I may say they do appreciate your management of, what is it?'

He glanced down at his iPad, 'Twenty-seven ladies in the Secretariat. But you see when I get a letter like this from a husband I, we, have to discuss the matter.'

Aubrey read the letter out once again in which the husband claimed that his wife's, Mary's breast cancer treatment required more time off than had been initially envisaged, and the extended time-off request, was being questioned by his wife's manager who had indicated that his wife's role as Section Supervisor would be down-graded if the additional time was taken.

'A matter,' continued Aubrey, 'Which Mary's husband says has caused his wife a great deal of stress at a very difficult time in her life.'

Geraldine sighed and said, 'If I didn't encourage breast cancer patients in my team to keep active whilst they go through their treatment you would be forever trying to find me new staff members. Remember, I have had five girls from my team with breast cancer in the last two years and one way or the other they are all still working for the company.'

'I know, I know,' said Aubrey wearily, 'But look could I tell this husband you will keep Mary on her supervisory grade if she shows she makes every effort to come in during her treatment?'

Aubrey was almost pleading at this point.

'OK, OK, but don't blame me if I have to ask for another junior girl to cover during the time we have to go through the chemo process.'

Back in her office, looking through the window at the neat ranks of desks with the girls bending towards their computers, Geraldine felt a warm glow of satisfaction at the sight of the "best run" department in the company, according to the Group Chairman at his last annual staff statement to the whole insurance company workforce standing obediently, wall to wall, in the canteen. All listening intently for the point where the Chairman cleared his throat and announced 'the annual bonus percentage this year will be…'

Back in her studio flat that evening Geraldine watched the television BBC News where an item on the growing concern over the higher percentage of women reporting cancer problems caught her attention, reminding her that her Senior Supervisor, Mary, was one of the statistics.

A little disturbed by the meeting with the HR Manager and the News, she considered doing a training run for an hour to clear her mind despite the fact that this was not on her training schedule for the half marathon she was looking forward to running in two weeks.

Still somewhat bothered, Geraldine abandoned the thought of a training run, excusing herself by noting that a drizzle of rain was sliding down her window. She fell back on her personal therapy when bothered or bored by exercising her ‘keep on top and tidy’ attitude and turned to her desk and the file of old photos she had planned to put into an album. Thinking now that she was approaching fifty and without any close family, she should at least mark the various exciting and adventurous things she had accomplished in her life by recording dates and details with each photo. Compensation she knew for the space in her life which a family might have filled.

Photo after photo, hill walking, trekking, canoeing up the Amazon, a constant stream of reminders of her determined physical and outdoor activities were laid out on her desk.

Getting the photos of ‘her girls’ at one office event or another Geraldine comforted herself that the girls ‘liked her’ or at least, she thought, ‘respected’ her. An important view which sitting at the desk compensated a little for the loneliness she had come to notice more recently.

Once again she reflected back to the two or three men she had formed a physical, if not emotional association with, recognising now that each of them had been really looking for a ‘mother substitute’ and, thought

Geraldine, 'my positive style had sometimes appealed to them until they each bored or bothered me and then I had to send them on their separate ways.'

That evening standing in the shower, she checked again the slight protrusion on the lower side of her left breast, pleased to feel no real change from the first time she had noticed the slight lump six or so months before.

None the less as she dried herself and prepared for bed she decided to do a little research 'on Mary's behalf' she thought, anxious to separate herself from any thought of personal difficulty.

For more than an hour after following the links on her laptop on "breast cancer, things to know" Geraldine sat absorbing the range of issues raised by the subject. As she did so she began to realise for the first time that she had ignored any thought that she might be involved with cancer, feeling confident that her lifestyle and physical condition running and training, plus her strength of mind and professional responsibilities, the bedrock of her self-confidence, left her certain that she could fight off any illness.

Now as she absorbed the information on the process of breast x-rays, ultra sound scans, fine needle core biopsy, all directed to early diagnosis, and the emphasis on the importance of information to establish whether the cancer from the breast had spread via the lymph nodes and on to other parts of the body, Geraldine left her bed and laptop and returned to the bathroom mirror.

She saw no redness around the lump nor could she feel any swelling under her armpit, however, before she returned to bed she determined to check with her doctor for an appointment.

Geraldine's call next morning to the doctor's surgery received an immediate response and an appointment three days later to the Breast Cancer nurse at the surgery. Spurred on by the step she had taken she phoned Mary's home from her office. Mary answered with a very weary voice and when Geraldine had observed the pleasantries and asked how Mary was, and finding that Mary's response was to emphasise the weariness she felt because of the chemo, Geraldine offered to pop round that very afternoon, surprising herself and Mary by the proposal.

Mary had set out her best tea set and napkins in her front room and was clearly nervous that her boss was visiting. Geraldine equally found it quite difficult to sit and chat with Mary, who was more used to a business briefing between the two of them conducted every day rather formally in Geraldine's office.

After a rather stilted quarter of an hour over the teacups, Geraldine fell back on questioning Mary on the status of her breast cancer and was then rather caught out by the detail and complexity of the chemo treatment to shrink the tumour.

'The first phase of my hair loss is beginning to show,' said Mary, tweaking her attractive blonde hair and explaining the importance of finding the cancer had not spread to her lymph glands and beyond.

As Geraldine left Mary's house, she had no difficulty in saying 'Take what time you need' and 'of course I will keep your supervisory role open for you. Please tell your husband', and on her drive home she realised how much better she felt for conducting the meeting as she had.

Events took Geraldine along on a 'conveyor belt' of inspection tests as the breast cancer medical procedures suddenly dominated Geraldine's days and her thinking. Her urgent request to see Aubrey Livingstone to ask for time off was acutely embarrassing in view of previous meetings, although Aubrey rather loftily agreed to her being away for some days without a clear schedule of the times. She had the feeling he was rather pleased to "grant" her the arrangements, "maintaining" as he said "the active cultural understanding we like to pursue in the company."

Geraldine realised their relationship would never be the same again.

The mammogram followed by the MRI and several biopsies as medical issues took a hold on her life, within days Geraldine found herself in the Specialist's room as he said, 'I think you should have a mastectomy and I strongly suggest we start a programme of chemotherapy. I am giving you a prescription for pre-chemo anti-sickness pills which I suggest we get started on as soon as possible.'

Back in the office Geraldine's absences and the reasons for it had become common knowledge and even in her rather shocked state she realised that her ladies' attitude had somehow changed.

A few evenings later as Geraldine was trying to come to terms with having to cancel her half marathon and face up to the approaching removal of her breast, when the phone rang. It was Mary.

'Geraldine it was really nice of you to bother about me when I was feeling so low and now I hear what you are going through I thought I could repay your kindness by inviting you over to our little 'breast support' evenings. Five of your ladies and I meet regularly to back each other up. We have tons of details about clothes, bras, pick-you-ups, special wigs. You would be surprised what we have come up with and we have lots of laughs.'

Mary continued, 'Would you come over and be with us as we would all love it if you would?'

Geraldine managed to reply, 'I would love to,' and gently put the phone down in floods of tears. Finally, she realised she was not on her own!

THE FIRST SPEECH

'Look Johnny you will just have to help, after all it's only introducing the raffle.' Johnny leaned back on the step ladder to make sure the nails he had just tapped in were at the same level from the roof as the other side of the banner across the top table proclaiming, "The Children's Refuge Charity Supporters Dinner".

Johnny backed down the three steps, carefully and slowly, delaying the inevitable moment when he would have to face his determined wife who was impatiently taping her foot awaiting his arrival.

'Look, Mabel' was as far as he got before Mabel once again said:

'All the committee ladies are fully involved during the evening as you very well know. Besides me all have worked so hard to get a celebrity TV personality to come and say a few words when we launch the raffle, beginning with Tommy Tarrent the TV news reader who only lives down the road but despite my efforts, our efforts, everyone had one lame excuse or another for not being able to support us. So the committee agreed one of the husbands should stand in, and as Vice-Chair I naturally volunteered you.'

'Naturally,' said Johnny heavily, 'Only I have never made a public speech. I am just not suited. I am, well, shy and look always do things like this for the committee' he exclaimed, waving his hammer at the wall 'and all the printing and the clearing up.'

Mabel cut him short. 'Everyone knows that, which is why I volunteered you and you can't let me down in front of ten ladies in this town. I would never live the embarrassment down. I would have to resign and I was a founder member. You must know somebody who could help you say a few words to get the raffle going?'

Johnny's sleep was disturbed by seeing himself on a stage before hundreds of people all staring at him whilst his mouth opened and closed when no words came out.

In the pub the next evening getting his usual pint before he went home, he confessed his acute anxiety to Reg, the landlord.

Reg, ever helpful to his customers particularly his regulars, ready to give advice on any anxiety they may have from the likely winners at the Aintree Grand National, dealing with disruptive children or awkward bosses, and regularly, very awkward wives as well as the everyday issues which cross the bar day in and day out.

Reg mulled things over before saying, 'Why don't you talk to Spike at the second-hand car place on the Green. He has a lovely line in patter. God knows how many people he has convinced to buy one of his motors, even when it was the last thing on their minds!'

Johnny thought about this suggestion and went straight down to the Faircar Exchange forecourt on his way home and asked to see Spike.

Spike greeted him like a long lost relative.

'Johnny, great to see you, you were just on my mind. That old motor of yours is really on its last legs and I have just the guy who could help you out in a trade-in, and just yesterday I had this dear old lady bring in a lovely little Nissan as she no longer wants to drive. Hardly any mileage and we have serviced it for her for years.'

Johnny managed to disrupt the flow of patter by waving his hands, 'No, no, I am not here about changing my motor. Reg up the pub thought you might help me with a little problem I have.'

'Best see a doctor, not me,' guffawed Spike loudly.

'No, it's nothing like that,' said Johnny, 'I have to make a speech, well introduce the raffle at the Children's Refuge Charity Supporter's Dinner up at the Coronation Hall on Saturday and I am hopeless at making speeches. Well, I've never made a speech, and Reg thought you might give me some ideas.'

'Oh sure, no problem at all. Let's see now, Johnny, mixed audience all feeling a bit posh on the evening. No peas on a knife stuff! Few bevies before and I suppose the tickets include a glass or two of wine?'

'Well yes, wine is provided,' said Johnny.

'Excellent, everyone will be nicely oiled for your speech. Now here are one or two of my best jokes you can use. OK buy me a beer when I see you next time up at the Lamb and Duck,' continued Spike, warming to the challenge.

Spike then recounted several ribald jokes, insisting Johnny wrote down a gist of each as he laughed his way noisily through each story, until he said 'There you go Johnny boy, just give those to the gathered throng and when they have stopped laughing just say, "OK girls and boys, open up the wallets and handbags and snap up the raffle tickets before they all go," and you will have sorted your speech – big time.'

That evening Johnny stared bleakly at his computer screen at various headings.

"Guide to Efficient Speech Making"

"Presenting a speech – five steps"

"Speaking and audience management"

All of which had left him completely confused, his head aching with jargon, buzz words, marker points, on and on, until he sat back in a state of anxious despair with still no plans for the next day's Saturday speech.

Saturday morning dawned and after an almost sleepless night Johnny was up early and on his way to the Children's Refuge Centre, as he did almost every Saturday morning, to carry out the never-ending list of minor maintenance jobs that were essential to keep the centre ticking over. The staff working in the seven twenty-four hour unit, happy as they took to the well-being of the five, often disturbed and frequently unhappy children, whose lives showed its unfair side to them at a very early age.

Sarah, the Matron, met him as usual with a smile and a cup of tea before giving him a short list of items that she hoped he might tackle, avoiding the need to bring in outside professionals that inevitably added to the stretched cost of running the centre.

'And,' said Sarah, 'The boiler seems to be on the blink again, just as the weather is getting colder.'

Johnny collected his tool set and unlocking the cellar door, went down the steps to where the elderly Potterton boiler resided. He had just decided to take the control panel cover off, when he realised he wasn't on his own.

Sitting silently behind him on the bottom step of the concrete stairs was Peter, a ten-year-old resident, small for his age, who quite often joined him on his Saturday morning rounds.

'Now, Peter, you know Matron would be mad with both of us if she found you down here. You know this cellar is supposed to be out of bounds,' Johnny said gently to the small boy.

Peter, ever serious, nodded looking up at Johnny with his large expansive eyes in a face made more pale than usual by the illumination from the single light bulb dangling above the boiler.

Johnny smiling down on Peter's serious face said, 'OK as you are here make yourself useful and dig out my biggest screwdriver from the tool box there.'

Peter, who rarely spoke when they were together but was ready to help with tools or holding things for Johnny, swiftly found the screwdriver and handed it, handle forwards, to Johnny as Johnny had showed him to do.

Unscrewing the plate took time and Johnny found himself telling Peter, who remained sitting in silence on the step, about his difficulties in having to introduce the raffle without anything to say, and his anxieties in having to stand up before all the people to say anything at all.

Peter sat motionless with his arms around his knees, staring up intently at Johnny as the one-sided conversation continued.

Johnny finished his tale of concern, got the panel off and started to inspect the fuses one by one. The silence was broken by Peter.

'Why don't you just tell them the truth about this place and us?'

Not only was this sentence far longer than any previously shared by the ten-year-old but its content seemed completely at odds to anything Johnny imagined would be within the thinking processes of the little lad on the stairs.

After clearing his throat and looking down at Peter for a moment, Johnny said.

'You mean giving them a bit about you, and what the ladies do for you, well, all of you?'

Peter's 'Yes,' was positive and Johnny said. 'Well, OK, what should I say about you?'

'Well,' said Peter, without moving or changing his expression, 'Just say, I was not wanted by my mum who was bashed about by my dad, who was always drinking and when the court took me into care the man said it would save me from being bashed about.'

'The ladies here are OK 'cos mostly they listen to you and they let me keep my bits and pieces in my own locker, which is more than I ever had at home. And Matron said I am doing alright at school. Tell them that.'

Johnny sat down next to Peter on the step, 'I'm going to say just what you have told me and then I am going to get back here tomorrow and tell you how it went.'

The Dinner went smoothly and coffee and mints arrived into the atmosphere made comfortable by good food and convivial conversation.

Mabel had almost asked Johnny if he had his speech several times and only thought the better of it because Johnny was strangely silent and seemed unperturbed by the occasion, and to her considerable surprise had not asked her for support for his contribution. Indeed, he had hardly spoken during the dinner and appeared to be enjoying the meal.

Mabel was even more surprised as the plates were being cleared before coffee, when Johnny left his seat and their guests, without comment, and walked across the floor to the table where the raffle items had been gathered.

Johnny had a fork in his hand and an empty wine glass.

The sound of a wine glass vibrating to the fork cut through the hubbub with dramatic effect and the room stilled.

Johnny said, ‘Before I let you loose on the raffle I want to tell you a little story.’ He then gave them verbally word for word what Peter had said to him, adding how uplifting it was for him to see these damaged youngsters find their characters and their confidence in the home.

In the emotional silence at the end of his speech, a voice said, ‘I am sorry I am late after your committee’s invitation, but I have just got back from a flight from the USA an hour ago, but having listened to your speaker’s marvellous descriptive introduction on the work of the Home, that has clearly moved everyone including me, there was really no need for my contribution.’

This said, Tommy Tarrent moved out of the shadows at the back of the hall to applause all round.

Tommy held up his hand for silence, 'I am going to invite your speaker to join me tomorrow on the TV evening show to repeat his story, which I know will fascinate and catch the emotions of my national audience and I am absolutely sure the Charity will benefit from the interest that your fine speaker this evening will generate on my show.'

SHIPS IN THE NIGHT

Harry Rathbone and Will Prentice had known each other all their lives, their families lived in the same street in East Grinstead. They had moved through the local school system, class after class, and after a brief period into the further education structure in an attempt to achieve some academic accreditation, both had given up education under the disappointed gaze of their parents and joined local general trades, Will into house clearance and Harry was taken on by the main second-hand furniture store in the town.

During the years they emerged and shaped themselves from junior school into an adult earning life, each with motor cycles and then second-hand motors, with partners, children and marriage. Keeping in step at each phase without preplanning other than the matching sequence governed by luck. Neither did they at any stage share their experiences.

They would, and did, deny they were friends, just acquaintances and saw each other irregularly. Will supported his East Grinstead Football Team, reliably weak and generally to be found in the bottom third of the South East League, whilst Harry supported the local cricket team whose performance season after season was much the same.

Harry even made a radical career adjustment at much the same time and they acquired leases, number 101 High Street and 61 in the same main thoroughfare in the town within three months of each other to set up their own Antique businesses. Prompted into this out of character action by their wives who had absorbed the facts from television programmes which were highlighting the new trend of antiques. Buying, collecting and selling all created an exciting growth market and some expectation of financial benefit for each family.

The two wives met quite regularly and in addition to their children's welfare and schooling found much in common including the nonsensical distance their Husbands kept from each other, a distance based upon an earlier incident in the school playground when Will had accused Harry of stealing his bicycle pump. A story subsequently disproved when the school's most active pickpocket was brought before the Magistrate by the Police following the discovery of eight stolen bicycles and forty-one bicycle pumps, but by this point the damage had been done between Will and Harry.

The buying and selling opportunities presented by the television programmes encouraged people to clear their lofts and cupboards of unwanted items in the hope they would find a valuable antique where the local antique shop was an acceptable avenue for selling off unwanted items, and if they proved to be 'collectables,' rather than antiques, that still might add to the family holiday fund or mortgage payments.

Both Harry and Will's Antique and Collectable shops prospered in a modest way, particularly where they were able to trade based upon their furniture and house clearance experiences.

Time moved on and the antique trade became more competitive and the number of shops in every town increased. Will and Harry found themselves approaching retirement, trying to manage a single-handed practice, worried about the future.

Once again behind the scenes planning by their wives, also worried about the future, forced the cards playing side up, on to the table.

All four met one evening in the High Street fish and chip shop for chips and a chat.

The girls introduced their 'plan' to the two men who were sitting silently with folded arms as they explained that a large furniture sales room at number 96 in the High Street was empty.

'Why can't you two share the premises, saving the cost of your own sites and each work three days of the week so that you can both spend more time with the family?'

The wives were organised and firm and without anywhere to go both husbands agreed and shook hands over the vinegar bottles.

Although cautious at first, both Harry and Will saw the sense in the new arrangements and within six months and a coat of paint, the Cooperative Antique Centre was opened with a fanfare in the local paper and with Will and Harry standing arm in arm in front of their joint shop window, stuffed with collectables and the odd one or two actual antiques. The newspaper shot even had the suspicion of a smile on their faces!

The three-day working Monday, Wednesday and Friday, then Tuesday, Thursday and Saturday alternating the days every month worked smoothly.

It was only after three months when the accumulated boxes and bags of collectables and antiques, brought together in something of a rush from their old premises and stored in the cavernous back storeroom of the antique shop, did the problem arise.

Harry was clearing and sorting one of the boxes on a quiet Tuesday. The two men had agreed to sort the boxes and bags row by row and take the best items, or the most potentially saleable items, through to the front shop area where the following day the partner would decide where to place the item in the most appropriate location in the shop.

This harmonious arrangement was helped by the working agreement Will and Harry had come to in which they agreed to halve the running cost and halve the investment cost for buying in new items to sell in the shop.

Both men had agreed that they would commit up to fifty pounds for any item they thought worth investing in, but discuss any items considered to have a higher value with each other before making a commitment.

The money management procedure had worked well and the net profit, which they shared equally at the end of the first month, was very encouraging. So much so that they went to the Bull's Head and to the surprise of the landlord and the bar leaners, shared a couple of pints together.

The Tuesday problem arose when Harry found a small leather embossed box in a box of assorted items that included a wooden set of bookends in an antique horn inkwell set, a dozen schoolbooks, a First World War tin helmet and a quantity of brick-a-back without any obvious value.

The embossed box was different and upon opening it, Harry discovered a beautifully ornate gold finger ring with figuring all the way round. Whilst he was unsure of the age, Harry was sure the ring was of considerable age and had to be an antique of value.

Harry decided to find out more about the ring and in the meantime say nothing about it to his partner, a shifty decision about which he felt a little guilty.

The following morning in the usual 'cup of tea' handover Harry identified the other items, including several schoolboy items and the wooden bookends, indicating he was fairly sure it was from one of the boxes he had brought into the joint business.

Will, busy placing the items about, gave no real thought to where the items had originated, all too conscious that the back storage room was still half full of boxes and bags that needed to be sorted and displayed.

A couple of days later Harry was able to show the antique ring to an old mate in the antique jewellery trade who immediately told him, having spent a few minutes looking at the ring through his eyeglass, that the ring could have 'royal connections' having inspected the figuring around the circumference and he advised Harry to take his ring to a specialist dealer for reference.

Excited but somewhat anxious, Harry left the ring with the antique jewellery sales company whose expert had indicated that subject to further investigations, the ring could have a three figure value. He promised that Harry would get a call in a couple of days with a specific indication of value at auction, and a sales day when the ring might be presented and its sale promoted.

That night Harry found himself overwhelmed by the excitement and the anxiety of being made several thousand pounds better off, and he shared his secret with his wife. She was less than impressed with his self-interested actions but her first question was, 'Are you sure you brought the ring in from your place?'

'Oh, pretty sure, well yes, very sure. That's why I thought we should benefit,' said Harry, weakly.

The very next meeting all four met at the Centre and a now crestfallen Harry explained, under the very firm eye of his wife, that he had found an antique ring in a box of general stuff he had brought in from one of his old customers and, 'Without realising its value had gone to an antique jewellery expert to get a value so that we could make a decision as to what to do!'

Will gave Harry a 'bicycle pump' stare and his wife said to break the silence, 'Well let's go and look at this famous box in case there is anything else worth having?'

In the store room the four stood around the box and Will said positively, 'I brought this box in,' pointing at a named label on side, 'I remember it well.'

Harry leapt in, 'Gosh, sorry Will, my mistake, thought it was one of mine with all that other junk. Anyway now we can all decide how to deal with the sale money. You know 50-50, same as always.'

The relief of getting this out almost caused Harry to laugh with joy.

Will said, 'This was a nasty box', which caused the other three to focus their attention in his direction.

'I remember this old lady coming into the store and asking me what I would charge to clear her house of unwanted stuff as she was going to live with her sister for what time she had left. I explained it would depend on what items of value I could sell and I went round to see what was what and to give her an estimate.'

Will continued, 'There were a few bits of saleable furniture, one or two carpets and some stored rubbish, old suitcases and this box in the roof. The old lady told me the box was her son's, her only relative and he was in prison and would be for, I think she said ten years.'

'I took a brief look into the box and saw nothing of value and certainly nothing that suggested it was the haul from a burglary, and I have not bothered to check the contents ever since.' Will concluded.

'Was he in for ... er ... murder or anything like that?' Harry asked anxiously.

'Not sure but ten years is a long stretch and he must be still there,' replied Will.

At that moment the phone in the store rang and Harry picked it up. 'Yes, this is Harry Rathbone. Yes, I did bring in the gold … oh it is a Royal ring, a 'Mourning Ring' Seventeenth century and worth what?! Stolen. OK, goodness … it's the "Middlewick" ring. Quite famous, I suppose it must be,' said Harry. 'Stolen five years ago … you say! Oh, you have returned it to the Museum and they were delighted. So glad you did that,' said Harry, looking at the other three as he continued the conversation. 'What a relief, as we wondered about it of course. So the police will be calling you say to see if we can shed any light on the theft. Well I assure you we will help them anyway we can. Thank you so much for calling. We were very anxious as to where the ring had come from and how we should deal with it. Thank you … goodbye.'

Harry put the phone down and there was a lengthy pregnant, silence before Harry's wife said, 'Thank goodness for that. Just suppose we had tried to sell the ring and then the fact that it had been stolen would have come up, our name would have been mud. We are doing all right as we are.'

And with that the two girls left.

Harry looked at Will and said, 'They're right, we are doing OK. Come on I will buy you a pint at the Bull's Head and we can get our "helpful" story together for when the police chap arrives.'

TAKING ON THE IMMIGRANTS

Arnold Culpeper, MBE, was at the kitchen table reading *The Times* whilst having his breakfast. When his wife had been alive he was never allowed this indulgence but he had become accustomed to the tea and toast prepared at eight each morning, whilst *The Times* delivered earlier gave him the information he needed to comment loudly and vociferously every time an item that displeased him caught his eye.

Arnold's comments were not directed specifically, generally being of a random nature. One of the problems of his gathering age and his communication style which, although he never accepted the reasons, had caused his abrupt retirement as a Magistrate on the local Bench rather than allowing him as he wanted, and expected, to have a second term in office.

It was well rumoured that the Chairman of the Bench had said.

'We really cannot have Culpeper continuing his interminable tirades on the Bench any longer.'

The recipient of his breakfast discourse on the world and its worries from *The Times* was as usual Magdalena, his Polish daily who came every morning, Monday to Friday, to tidy up, fix breakfast and prepare something for his supper.

Magdalena spoke English very well, having been living in the United Kingdom for some ten years and had taken up the job with Arnold Culpeper soon after his wife had passed away, thanks to his sudden realisation soon after his wife's passing that he needed somebody to help in the house.

Arnold had tried several local ladies who had all turned the job down only one lasting more than a week, thanks to his irascible and demanding style.

Finally, in some desperation he had turned to an agency who had introduced the newly arrived Magdalena, who at that point spoke almost no English and understood even less, having recently arrived from Poland. However, over the years she acquired a perfectly good level of English language skills but ignored Arnold Culpeper's constant breakfast comments and complaints by pretending she did not understand.

The situation, as normal on this particular morning as Magdalena swept the kitchen floor, shifting Arnold's feet unceremoniously under the table with the head of the broom, he enjoyed his toast, two pieces and his traditional chunky marmalade with his several cups of strong tea.

In truth, and privately, Arnold acknowledged he needed and valued Magdalena's support and her tolerance, and he rather enjoyed reading out *The Times* items and giving her his impressions, comments, objections and just occasionally his support, fondly imagining she would not really understand the English ways coming from Poland!

Arnold Culpeper frequently commented when the matter of immigration arose in conversation at the Conservative Club where he was wont to take lunch on most days of the week with his small group of retired cronies all from the local business community.

'You cannot expect anyone coming to this country from the European Union to understand the cultural, legal and political sophistication which centuries have bred into the English people's way of life,' was the mantra Arnold frequently used.

'And there are too many of these immigrants anyway.' A theme which always accorded well with the lunch group, particularly after they enjoyed a glass or two of whisky.

The difficulty of recruiting local people to help serve in the dining room at the Conservative Club had been a growing issue for some time and the Club had turned to agencies offering EU staff and this had led to some confusion over interpretation over lunch menus where Lamb chops sometimes would turn up as Ham and chips or Pork cutlets turn up in the form of Pot Noodles.

The situation had built up to such a crescendo of almost daily verbal complaint from Arnold Culpeper's group and a steady flow of the overseas waiters leaving the Conservative Club employ until the day when the

General Manager of the Club, together with the Chairman of the Members' Committee arrived at the usual table where Arnold and his three-man group were seated and advised them in no uncertain terms.

That, 'Any further complaints directed at the staff would be taken by the Committee as a clear indication that the four were "unhappy" with the service the Conservative Club provided and their membership would therefore be terminated forthwith.'

The event caused much merriment and general support from the membership. Arnold Culpeper and his cronies chose discretion over valour and, driven by fear of being barred from the Club, took to communicating with the Waiting staff in studiously civil terms careful to avoid any reference to their poor English or failure to catch their specific menu request. They achieved this by speaking with an exaggerated slowness and frequently indicating with a pointed finger the items on the menu card.

No such care was required in Arnold's morning tirade in which Magdalena showed not the slightest interest, no matter what the subject was, including a politician's inability to manage his or her area of responsibility, the NHS, the Education system, the state of the refuse collections, and the handling of the various Middle East conflicts. The subject that came in for particular criticism although Magdalena was supposed to notice, albeit silently, was the English Cricket Team, players and management all receiving the same abuse.

One particular morning the banner headline, as it had been for some time, was the deteriorating and ever growing need to deal with the EU's immigration crisis.

'And,' said Arnold, largely to the wall as Magdalena washed up the dishes, 'what can you expect when the door is opened to thousands of immigrants looking for a better life from Africa at the same time as these people fleeing conflict in Syria, and no proper border controls. This country cannot afford to take everyone in.'

'Look at this.' Arnold stabbed the paper with his finger.

'Three hundred thousand have crossed the Mediterranean from Africa seeking a better life in Europe. No wonder when they get muddled up with the real refugees from Syria, nobody knows one from another.'

Magdalena concentrated on drying the teacup without showing any sign of interest.

At the end of her shift tidying Arnold's house, Magdalena found him in his garage and said, 'See you tomorrow,' to his backside as he teetered over trying to wash the base of the wheels on his much cherished old Rover saloon car.

Hearing her goodbye Arnold slithered about thanks to the soapy water on the drive, but saved by Magdalena's firm hand under his arm.

'Oh, oops, thanks Magdalena, don't know what I would do without you. Keeping the old lady clean is getting a bit much for my dodgy hip.'

'I find you good man, clean every week. You want?' enquired Magdalena.

'Well, if you know someone Magdalena, send him over and I will give him a try,' said Arnold as he continued ineffectually to clean his treasured possession.

So it was that a Syrian immigrant, qualified accountant desperate for work, knocked on Arnold's door a week later and in broken, but understandable English, explained that Magdalena had asked him to come to try for the car-cleaning role.

He had been carefully prepared by Magdalena to say the right things to Arnold Culpeper with several mentions of 'professional' even though there was little relevance to his trained experience and this job, and intermingled his introductions with 'Sir' on several occasions.

Arnold, who was bothered about his deteriorating hip and hated the thought of being seen driving in a muddy Rover agreed to a trial.

The following week Kosia Halder brought his son Jay with him to practise his vocabulary. This bright ten-year-old already had two terms in the local school and with very firm instructions from his father as to how he should address Arnold Culpeper, a Member of the British Empire, followed his script carefully and impressed the ever gullible ex-Magistrate in doing so.

The cleaning process went 'sparkling' to the point that Arnold passed a tip, small but a tip none the less, to Jay when he paid Kosia for the visit.

Several weeks went by and Magdalena found occasion to explain that the Haldar family were struggling to establish themselves and were determined to do so after the ethnic pressures and problems they had experienced in Syria.

The weekly ritual became important to Arnold who found Jay's informative chats on the school and his gathering interest in British Classic cars and sport very engaging to the point that he prepared for their chats with the odd bag of sweets.

Six months later Arnold was seated with a strangely silent Jay in front of a glass of lemonade when Jay said.

'This is our goodbye week, we can come no more. My dad cannot get accounting work so he not get Government license to stay in England, so we must go back to Syria.' and this said the little lad burst into tears.

Arnold was horrified and calling out to Magdalena for tissues asked her if she knew about the situation.

Later when he had time to think about it, Arnold was surprised that Magdalena spoke to him in such detail and so clearly in flowing English.

Having listened to Magdalena explaining the problem, Arnold got a pen and notebook and asked Kosia to stop cleaning the Rover while he concentrated on the details of the imminent crisis of the Halder family having to leave England.

It became quickly clear to Arnold that unless Kosia received a job offer in an Accounting firm within the next week, the Immigration Department would rescind his temporary work visa and he would be deported.

Arnold rallied his team that very morning at the Conservative Club, emphasizing the injustice in the impending deportation and feeding details of the importance of having a young vigorous increase in working people paying taxes to offset the traditional ageing UK population.

He did so to such a degree that several members of the Conservative Club gathered around, and the general attitude from the gathering was that, 'Since you are trying on a humanitarian basis to help this worthwhile family perhaps we can also help.'

Ten minutes later Michael Wyman, whose brother was a Senior Partner in a sizeable local Accounting practice, put a name, address and an interview time on a piece of paper into Arnold's hand.

So it was three days later with Magdalena and Arnold in support, Kosia Halder received a six months' contract to work as an accountant in the firm.

Arnold lost his car cleaner but earned the devoted support of Magdalena and from then on had real discussions over breakfast in the mornings about items in *The Times*.

Much more importantly to Arnold was when he found himself sitting proudly in the school assembly hall with the Halder family when Jay was called forward to receive the Year Class Prize for English Language.

A LITERARY HAIRCUT

Nick Brown arrived precisely at 10.25 a.m. for his bi-weekly hair trim, stopping to note his reflection in the Burlington Arcade Military Regalia shop opposite the hairdressers as he always did, before making a quite unnecessary adjustment to his military insignia tie.

Nick reminded himself he should come down a little earlier on his next visit and pick up a couple more military ties to add to his considerable collection, perhaps the Black Watch colours, as he pushed the door embossed specifically as a 'Gentleman's Hairdresser' and entered Carlos's salon.

Carlos greeted him, as always, in his enthusiastic Italian way.

'Ah, good morning Nick, how is the famous writer and adventurer this fine morning?'

'I am well and as busy as ever, Carlos, and I need to look my best as I am off to your fair country tomorrow for a few days to finish my next book called *Nightmare in Patagonia* in my favourite hotel in Jessolo, away from all the noise and confusion here in London.'

Carlo clapped his hands in delight.

'Moto bene,' how I envy you and will you pay a visit to my beautiful Venice while you are there?'

'Well I expect so. It is a fine place with its history and culture to get some ideas for my next novel,' replied Nick.

Carlos enquired, 'No time to do a little trekking and climbing in the mountains while you are in Italy? I know how important it is for you to keep those adventurous experiences on the edge which makes your books so alive and popular.'

'I was telling my next client all about your adventurous life and your marvellous adventure books. He was most impressed and interested and wanted to meet you, not surprising as he is something in the TV business.'

Carlos, as professional as ever during the exchanges, had Nick's jacket off, seated him with his back to the washbowl, his tie loosened and collar undone, with a white towel neatly fitted around his neck.

Carlos was rubbing shampoo into Nick's hair as he leaned comfortably back over the bowl when the salon door opened and a dapper gentleman stepped inside.

'Ah, good morning, Gerald, how nice to see you. May I introduce the great adventurer and writer Nick Barrington-Brown I was telling you about and Nick this is Gerald Smythe, Chief of the ACE Television company.'

The ‘good mornings’ collided across the salon and Gerald Smythe settled into a seat by the low table with neatly placed *Times* newspaper and a range of *Country Life* style magazines.

Ever the conversationalist, Carlo said to Gerald whilst using the hair dryer on Nick.

‘Nick is off tomorrow to finish his latest adventure book in my country.’

Carlos always referred to Italy as ‘my country,’ although he had been born and brought up in the East End of London as a third generation immigrant.

‘He stays near Venice in Jessolo but loves to visit his old haunts in Venice whilst he is there.’

‘Really,’ said Gerald, ‘How very interesting as I am preparing to have a TV programme on the history of Venice to be shown on BBC this Autumn and I was myself planning to go tomorrow to Venice, there and back in the day to pick up the draft script from a high up State official in the Venice legislature. Unfortunately, I had to change the plans this morning as I now have to go to New York for a meeting with CNN. They want me to do a series on the Security Services in London, a programme that would interest me a good deal.’

The discussion flowed comfortably as Carlos snipped and combed Nick’s hair into perfection, while Gerald expressed considerable interest in Nick’s adventure books and his adventurous life.

Nick found himself enjoying the exchanges and extended his stay with a cup of coffee from Carlos' Costa machine while Carlos weaved his scissors expertly, snipping and shaping Gerald's distinguished grey hair.

When Carlos had finished Gerald's hair, Nick and Gerald continued the friendly exchanges before Gerald said.

'Look, when we are both back in town, could we meet for lunch?' and proffering his card, he said, 'I don't know if you know Rules but I believe it's one of the best restaurants in London and has the great advantage of being a place where you can have a meal without being overheard, a rare spot in London.'

'I should be delighted,' said Nick, proffering his own rather elaborate, "Author and Adventurer" card.

Gerald then said, 'I know this is an awful presumption but do you think when you are in Venice you could possibly collect the draft script. Just an envelope, it will not be very big? I could get a messenger to deliver it to you wherever you are in the city on the day you decide to visit. You could then let me have it when I buy you lunch.'

Disarmed by Gerald's friendliness and the flattery he had received, Nick happily agreed to carry out the task and Gerald said he would text a meeting place and advise his Venetian contacts when Nick let him know what day he would be in the city.

It was on the British Airways flight from Gatwick to Venice the next day that Nick, armed with his second Business Class glass of champagne, suddenly realised this was the first real 'adventure' he had ever been on. The carefully crafted PR releases over the years from his Agent, Morton White, had ensured his adventure books were picked up and promoted, translated and made available in electronic formats in a dozen different languages without him having to move far from his office chair.

Nick recalled the latest Press release, "Nick Barrington-Brown traces the source of the Amazon River," that entailed three weeks with a native family in their dugout canoe, a stay that had generated a great deal of media coverage, according to Morton White.

We had in fairness, he remembered paddled across the Canyon Lake at Southsea Theme Park to provide a local journalist with a photo opportunity.

Slightly more than when he had climbed 3000 feet with his gear, and the hand gliding down in the Alps where it was promoted that he had spotted two climbers in difficulty and managed to land close to them and give first aid before he called up the Emergency Mountain Rescue Team, and then launched himself off the edge of a thousand foot cliff to complete his hand gliding trip to the village in the valley below.

Morton White, he recalled, had been very proud of this fictitious adventure.

Sitting in the plane and mulling over the various outrageous 'adventure' claims that Morton White had come up with and convinced him that they were essential if his adventure books were to 'get out there,' as he liked to remind Nick whenever Nick weakly tried to protest the exaggerated stories, and reviewing his 'adventurous life,' Nick reminded himself of the realities and was embarrassed to think back to when the Circle Line tube had been stuck mid station last month and the lights had gone off because of a power failure, he had very nearly wet himself.

He had never really got over being scared of the dark from his first and only cub scout camping night, when candles had been the only lights allowed and he had pleaded with his father on the phone to collect him the next day and how back at home his doting mother, who 'quite understood' his anxiety, promised he would never had to stay away again when there wasn't a light switch to turn on!

'Here I am,' thought Nick, 'Simple Nick Brown, an ordinary writer masquerading as Nick Barrington-Brown, Adventurer, and for the very first time in my life I am actually having a bit of an adventure. Can I see it through, he wondered, without making myself sick or having a heart attack?'

Steadying himself with a further glass of champagne, Nick almost convinced himself that all he had to do was meet a man and collect a script in an envelope and bring it back to London. What could be simpler and safer than that!

Casa Bianca Hotel was as comfortable and welcoming as ever, with the Hotel Manageress, Margaretta, showing him to his usual suite overlooking the immaculate private beach.

'We had your favourite writing desk Mr Barrington-Brown put into your suite, and I assure you none of our other guests will bother our distinguished writer guest during your stay over the next two days,' said Margaretta as she quietly closed the door.

Somehow the writing did not flow as it usually did encouraged by good Italian food and wine and Nick found himself continuously bothered, even dreading, his errand for Gerald Smythe, so much so that he decided to leave the collection of the letter until he was on his way to the airport for his return flight to London.

On the morning of his final day in Italy, Nick texted Mr Smythe that he was ready to pick up the script and would have an hour in Venice that afternoon before he would need to get to the airport for the evening flight.

The response from Gerald was almost instantaneous.

'Would you be so kind as to stand by the entrance to the Palazzo Ducal on the edge of the Piazza San Marco any time between four and five in the afternoon? The messenger bringing the script has a description of you and will approach with the envelope, but just to be absolutely sure the messenger will ask, "Do you have the time Sir?" and you should respond, "Do you mean UK time?" He will then pass over the script. If you could then bring the script back with you, I would be most grateful.'

Nick was somewhat intrigued by the message but thought no more about it as he packed his travel bag and prepared for his return to London.

Walking down Colle dei Fabbri into Piazza San Marco, Nick was surrounded by the flow of tourists who now invade Venice, brought in their thousands by the world's biggest cruise liners. Queues of Chinese, Japanese, American and Russian tourists obediently following the multitude of flags, signs and insignia hoisted aloft lot by the tour guides, who ushered and cajoled their bemused groups between one historic photo opportunity and another.

'How is anyone going to spot me,' thought Nick as he stood out of the sun in the arched doorway of the Palazzo Ducal, a building he recalled rather spookily had been the secretive centre of the city's political elite in historic times.

His reverie was broken by a slight man in a grey city suit who appeared from nowhere.

'Mr Barrington-Brown,' he said in perfect, if heavily Italian accented English.

'Indeed,' said Nick somewhat taken aback.

'Could you please tell me the time,' said the messenger.

'Do you mean UK time?' replied Nick to the script and the messenger slid a bulky envelope from the inside pocket of his suit and handed it to Nick, then disappeared into the crowd entering the Palazzo Ducal Museum as smoothly as he had arrived.

Nick pushed the envelope into his travel bag and went on his way to find a taxi for the airport, relieved the 'adventure' was over.

The flight was uneventful and the cab in London returned him to the prestigious Chelsea block, where he had his flat overlooking the river. The doorman acknowledged his return with a salute before saying.

'A gentleman was asking if you had returned from your visit to Italy this morning. Of course I said nothing and he did not leave a name.'

This news did not make Nick feel any more comfortable, adding to his disquiet over the whole envelope arrangement.

Nick entered his flat, shutting the door with some relief and he was just deciding where to put the envelope when his phone rang.

'Oh good evening Mr Barrington-Brown, I am PA to Mr Smythe of ACE TV. I was just enquiring if you managed to get our script home safely?'

'A funny choice of phrase' thought Nick, but he replied civilly enough.

'Yes, I have the envelope with me safe and sound.'

'Excellent, thank you so much. We will be in touch,' and the phone then went dead.

Nick walked about his flat wondering where to put the envelope until he could pass it over to Mr Smythe at their lunch at Rules.

Just holding the envelope made Nick thoroughly uncomfortable and he suddenly thought of his locker in the basement of the block of flats, and without more ado he let himself out of the flat and went through the entrance foyer down into the basement.

Putting in his code, Nick opened his No.9 safe box and spent a few minutes looking through the pile of papers and documents in the box before putting the envelope on top of the pile and shutting the lid of the box. He then made his way with a feeling of relief, back up the stairs and down the corridor towards his flat.

Walking down the carpeted corridor Nick suddenly had a sensation that something was amiss, and as he came up to his front door he saw it was slightly ajar.

Nick stopped and carefully thought through his actions when he had left the flat some thirty minutes earlier. He fingered the keys in his trouser pocket, certain that he had locked the door.

Pushing the door silently open Nick moved into his entrance hall and almost without thought he reached up and took down the Zulu Knobkerrie Club, hooked up on the wall with several other war-like African weapons he had placed to decorate the entrance, a feature that Morton White had insisted on as he said, 'It reminds every visitor of your adventurous lifestyle.'

Gripping the African club, he stood listening intently in the carpeted hallway until he heard slight sounds coming from his bedroom and he moved silently to the side of the door, his Knobkerrie club balanced in his right hand.

He suddenly realised that he really did know what had to be done as he had written about this sort of event dozens of times in his books.

The door was open and as he stood flat against the wall a heavy set man in a dark suit with a dark turtle neck sweater, holding a metal jemmy in front of him, came through the door. Seeing Nick standing in the hallway he began to raise the jemmy and Nick hit him on the side of the head with his African club.

The man dropped to the carpet without a sound.

Nick went into his bedroom, which was in some disarray with cupboards opened and drawer contents all over the floor.

Nick selected a silk tie from the twenty or so littered over the carpet, thinking as he did so he had never really liked the rather garish colour combination, before he returned to the intruder lying motionless face downward on the carpet.

Pulling the unconscious man's arms behind his back and knotting the silk tie tightly around the wrists until he was satisfied the intruder was confined, before fingering the man's pulse in his neck, satisfying himself that his heart was beating voluntarily and his airways were not constricted, Nick went into his lounge and phoned 999.

The call was answered instantly.

'Hallo, this is Barrington-Brown in Flat 15,' before the police receptionist said, 'A moment, Sir'.

A new authoritative voice said.

'This is M15, Sir. We will be with you immediately, stay where you are.'

Nick then heard a commotion in the corridor almost immediately and one, two and then three armed officers, machine pistols extended, moved smoothly into the flat, followed by a neatly suited gentleman with a clipped moustache, who strode over to where Nick stood.

'Mr Barrington-Brown. Gravesly of the Home Office, M15 Section,' he said, proffering his card.

'We are very grateful for your professional handling of this tricky situation. My men are just taking the intruder out now. You certainly dealt efficiently with him, we are sure he is one of the London Mafia cell we have been watching trying to recover the incriminating evidence in that TV script you were bringing back from Venice.'

'We will of course let ACE TV have a watered down version of the script when we have extracted all the really sensitive data and pass it on to the Italian Security Service, who asked us to help.'

Gravesly went on, 'The Mafia turncoat who provided the information, thanks to a considerable bribe by ACE, is apparently in safe custody in Rome really for his own health and safety. I have my technical people fixing new locks on your door as we speak and we are installing the latest CCTV surveillance cameras to the front and back of your block of flats.'

'We will, of course, be advising Mr Gerald Smythe of the situation,' he continued as he now glanced at his Brightling watch.

'I may add,' he said, warning Nick of the consequences of delving too deeply into Mafia or any other high-level organised crime.

'It was just as well they had someone of your experience and ability to help them out.'

'Well good day, Sir, and thank you again.' And with this and a firm handshake Gravesly left the room and moments later Nick heard the front door glide shut.

Walking thoughtfully back into his bedroom Nick was not entirely surprised to find all drawers and cupboard shut and the items immaculately replaced with the rather badly creased garish tie neatly placed on the dressing table.

'Damn,' thought Nick, 'I wished they had taken the wretched thing with them.'

The phone rang. It was Morton White's loud voice.

'Hi Nick, just checking you're back from your trip to Italy. I have had a great idea for your next PR release.'

Nick cut him short.

'Morton, I will call you for a meeting in a day or two but I'm going to make some changes to my marketing arrangements and I will be handling all PR releases myself in the future, so I will give you a call when I have finished my next book as I have one or two changes in mind.'

GROWN UP DECISIONS

Joe felt completely out of it sitting in the lawyer's office listening to the lawyer reading out his grandpa's bequests to the family in a dry as dust voice. His mother and father were smiling and relaxed already knowing they benefitted from the estate.

Joe's two older brothers seemed to be more interested in their next car race schedule and only stopped shuffling their saloon race car entry forms as the lawyer intoned dryly, 'Clive,' who looked up to hear he had a bequest of Ten thousand pounds which by the look on his face suggested his Ford would be getting a replacement engine.

The lawyer then called 'Vincent,' who was two years younger than Clive, but received the same bequest.

Joe could only think of his beloved grandfather whose loss he felt deeply as he sat there close to tears but gripping his handkerchief firmly in his pocket, determined not to shed a tear, conscious that at nineteen years would cause his older brothers to smirk and remind everyone the 'unwanted kid was blubbing again, why can't he grow up'.

Finally, 'To Joseph,' intoned the lawyer, 'I leave my trusty Morgan, two seater sports car and all the tools and equipment and boxes in its garage.'

On the way home in the car sandwiched between his brothers, the comments flew back and forth.

'Thought you were Grandpa's favourite; fancy leaving you that old wreck.'

'What are you going to do with her, sell her as soon as you can? She can't be worth much and let's face it you only got through your test, what a month ago? Better get yourself a Mini or a new bicycle'.

Joe became more and more defensive until their father ordered a stop to the one-sided bantering.

Back in their home that had for some years been shared with Joe's mother's father, Joe took the keys off the board and went down to the row of outhouses and lock up garages which the old house had in abundance, allowing the two brothers to spread their passion for racing a Ford Saloon car in the National Track series, with a monopoly over several garages.

Joe opened the door to the end brick built unit, immediately conscious of the smell and feeling of comfort as he entered his grandfather's 'inner sanctum,' as he liked to call it.

A commodious garage, lined with shelves with innumerable boxes with car parts marked up clearly with descriptions of the contents. 'Gear Ratios,' 'Brake Pads,' 'Sliding Sleeve Suspension'. Every part that a 1935 year old Flat Red Morgan might ever need surrounded the 'old lady' covered by a dust sheet in the middle of the garage floor.

Joe did not bother to stem the flow of emotions and tears as he stood with his hand on the dust sheet, remembering the times helping his Grandfather always busy with 'little jobs' on the Morgan. Telling stories of times and events that his grandfather had lived through during WW2 in London and then on as a conscripted National Service man, trained to be a vehicle mechanic, a skill Joe remembered him saying many times meant he then was able to build up his successful engineering business and provide for his family and acquire and look after the 'love of his life,' his Morgan, built in the year he was born.

Joe blew his nose noisily and pulled the dust sheet off the Morgan, looking at the car for the first time as its owner.

Navy Blue body work, the aluminium coach work polished and free from any chips and marks, how many times had his grandfather showed him how to prepare and touch in any stone chips. The cast aluminium wheels made by the Morgan Company, how many hours had he wire brushed the wheels and then blackened the tyres for his Grandfather, thought Joe.

The leather seats were well polished; another task Joe had done many times whilst his grandfather tinkered with the mechanics. Although looking once again at the two seats, Joe noticed they were a little 'tired' and creased with years of use, ‘In keeping with the car’ he could hear his grandfather’s voice.

At this point Joe realised there was an envelope with his name on it taped behind the steering wheel. Joe pulled it free and opening it found a single sheet of paper.

‘To my dearest grandson, Joe, in my Records box you will find the Log Book papers already transferred into your name. You have every right to sell the Morgan and you will benefit from a handy sum of money to help you along as you journey onwards.

If you decide to keep the Morgan, as I hope, you will also find one or two, hopefully, helpful notes in the box. I am only sorry she was not roadworthy so you could have driven her now you have passed your road test, but I am happy; I enjoyed your company many times in the car as we took our little trips and went to Morgan events.’

The letter went on, ‘You have given me great pleasure over the last nineteen years and I truly hope the Morgan will return the friendship for me, your Grandfather.’

Joe again blew his nose noisily, wishing he could have told his grandfather how much he loved and valued his calm comfort through some of those times when he had felt, “very much the late edition and not really wanted junior member of the family.”

Joe took down the wooden box marked ‘Records’ and put it on the bench where the tool rack held a multitude of shiny tools and implements collected by his grandfather over more than fifty years.

'Never have to look too far for the right tool here,' his Grandfather was fond of saying.

There were several bundles of papers and files all neatly tied with blue tape on top one of which was another envelope with his name on it.

"Dear Joe," read the letter, "As you know the Morgan has to have a road test and receive an MOT Certificate before you can drive and use, or should you decide to sell the 'old lady' to provide for the new owner. The only remaining task is to fit a new starter motor, the existing one is the original and the gearing has finally warn to the point it would not pass the MOT Inspector's test.

"I have left the instructions for fitting the new starter motor in the box with the unit (box marked 'Starter') but I suggest you give my old friend, Frank Corville, a call. You may remember we had lunch every week at the Working Mens' Club? Frank was a terrific motor mechanic and when I suggested you might need a bit of help to fix the starter motor, he was delighted. Give him a call, his number is on the label attached."

The following day, encouraged by their mother, Clive and Vince introduced a colleague of theirs in the Motor Sales business, Spike O'Shaunase, who immediately promoted his line to Joe, with a professionally disarming smile.

‘I can have a client ready to pay top dollar for your old Classic. Just give me half an hour with my camera and I will be back to you with a good offer. We will have it sorted in a week. Look, the boys help me with new clients thanks to their race motoring, so I will halve my usual commission rate as a favour for you. OK?’

Joe was somewhat taken aback by this ‘full frontal’ approach but he found himself saying,

‘Thanks a bundle, Spike. I am doing a bit of work on her, but once I have got her through her MOT I will give you a call, could you let me have your card!’

Spike obliged and apart from Joe’s mother suggesting he could have saved himself some trouble by ‘unloading the old crate,’ everyone seemed satisfied with the arrangement.

Frank came over within half an hour of Joe calling him the very next day and standing by the Morgan he told Joe his grandfather had said he might be of help and he would be delighted to work with Joe.

A couple of days later Joe and Frank had the Morgan bonnet cover off and with Joe holding the cable light and the Morgan supported on one side on a jack, so that the old starter motor on the right side of the engine was well exposed, Frank was able to slide under the Morgan’s steel chassis with ease, reminding Joe that with only four inches of normal road clearance, he would never have reached the unit without the lifting jack.

The old starter motor was out and the new unit bolted back in its place within the hour and they both stopped for a cup of tea before Frank insisted Joe gave the starter 'a twirl'.

Somewhat anxiously Joe seated himself for the first time "live" in the Morgan's driver seat, pressed the starter button and the motor turned and rumbled into life immediately.

'Right,' said Frank, 'It's time you gave this baby an airing,' and Joe drove the Morgan up and down the cul-de-sac passed their house once or twice, despite its illegal status on the road, with Frank watching approvingly on the pavement.

Before Frank left that evening he told Joe he would bring over some trade plates from the garage where he still helped out from time to time and arrange to have the garage carry out the MOT testing, Joe and Frank both being sure that Joe's grandpa had covered all the other aspects necessary to get the Morgan, old as she was, through the tests.

Joe was bursting with pride as he and Frank set off for the MOT test. His father and mother were on hand to see his first drive in "his" Morgan and even the brothers, who were still promoting the 'quick sale and get yourself a mini' argument came out from working on their Ford race saloon to watch the event.

As predicted the Inspector passed the old Morgan with flying colours, even commenting he saw cars two years from new which could not compete for the mechanical or electrical efficiency of the Morgan.

Joe and Frank both agreed that Grandpa would have been proud of the old lady's high standards as they drove home with the trade plates in the back of the Morgan.

Back in the garage Frank said to Joe,

'I guess you have a decision to make now?'

'I know,' replied Joe, 'And I'm not sure what Grandpa really wanted me to do. I know he wanted me to go on to University and get an engineering degree and I suppose he thought if I sell the Morgan, now it is fully operational, I would have sufficient money and perhaps a bit more to get me through the two years. I just feel pretty unsure what to do!'

'Didn't your Grandfather leave you a couple more envelopes in the "records" box?' enquired Frank. 'Before you finally decide perhaps you should look at those.'

'Of course I should,' said Joe, and he lifted down the box and put it on the workbench. Shifting the carefully taped up envelopes, Joe found the next envelope had, "To Joe, should you decide to sell," inscribed on it.

'Well I haven't,' said Joe, 'I just feel so undecided and I really want to do whatever Grandpa felt would be best for me'.

'Better open the envelope anyway,' said Frank. And so reluctantly Joe slit the envelope open.

'My dearest Grandson, now you have decided to sell the Morgan I would only ask you to get Frank's help to find a caring, experienced motor man as the new owner.

The money should get you through university and get you started in an engineering career – good luck.'

'Oh gosh, I just don't feel right about this, selling the Morgan, even though it seems Grandpa rather expected me to do that,' continued Joe in a subdued voice.

'Well then,' Frank said, 'I suggest you open the final envelope before you make your final decision.'

The final envelope simply said.

'It seems as if you are struggling to convince yourself to sell the Morgan whatever the pressures you are getting from the family. So here is what to do. Make an appointment to see the family lawyer again and take with you the new MOT Certificate.'

'Good grief, you cannot suppose the lawyer wants to buy the Morgan?' Joe said, with an incredulous look at Frank.

'Who knows, but you will only find out if you do what your Grandpa is suggesting,' came back Frank's gentle voice.

Three days later Joe found himself in his only suit sitting outside the lawyer's office door, reminding himself how miserable he had been on the last occasion he had sat in the seat.

The lawyer's secretary said, 'Please go into the office, he is expecting you now.'

The dry as dust voice said, 'Good morning Joe. I understand you want to talk to me about your Grandfather's bequest to you?'

'Well, I really don't know, but Grandfather left me a message that before I make my final decision about his bequest I should show you this.' Joe then placed the official MOT Certificate on the lawyer's desk.

The response was a broad smile, 'Well done, I am quite sure your grandfather had everything planned this way. He wanted you to really think about your future and I believe he was also safeguarding his most valuable and cherished possession, after his love for you. Now you have shown that you have the Morgan in full running order, I am authorised to tell you.'

"If you retain and maintain the Morgan, you will receive ten thousand pounds in quarterly payments every year until you choose to pass on the Morgan. Hopefully, as your Grandfather says here, to one of your children. In the meantime, you should be able to keep yourself comfortable at the University before you go on to have a successful career in engineering."

'Your grandfather continued,' said the lawyer with a smile.

"I am glad you struggled to work out the way forward and did not give in to others' pressures, and I hope you will drive the Morgan to Classic events and enjoy that side of your life, perhaps taking Frank with you. Just the way I hoped it would all work out for my favourite grandson."

AN INDEPENDENT YOUNG MAN

'How is your Mum today Andy?' asked Mr Hastings as Andy banged on the door to deliver the Saturday papers, together with the motorsport magazine Mr Hastings ordered every month from Cripps, the Newsagents on the corner.

'Come in and let's have a cup of tea,' said Mr Hastings, leading the way into his orderly kitchen, 'I have the kettle boiled' he continued, glancing at the huge wall clock over the Aga. 'I see you are two minutes late, it must be carrying that weight of papers!'

They both laughed as Andy's nine-fifteen arrival every Saturday and Sunday was carefully arranged as it had been for a couple of years to fit with Mr Hastings tea break, the time in the morning when he enjoyed a jam donut or some other little luxury which Andy's Mum could not often afford and certainly not now she has been forced to give up her part-time job.

'Now,' said Mr Hastings as Andy and he sat down at the washed wooden kitchen table. Andy's attention was on a larger than usual plate of cakes, several with chocolate icing sprinkled with coloured chocolate seeds, a favourite of Andy's, 'How is your mother?'

Andy grimaced as he said, 'Honestly not good, Mr Hastings. That nice nurse Ann at the Hospice said Mum is doing OK and is not in pain but she said we must not expect much now the cancer has spread like it has.'

Andy stared at his plate. The last six months had seemed like forever since his Mum was diagnosed with breast cancer.

'Mum says she is looking forward to seeing you this afternoon.'

'I'll be there as promised at the hospice. I will go in about four-thirty – we don't want her to get tired' replied Mr Hastings gently, 'Now get on with your cakes or I will have to be eating them all next week.'

'Now you stop that, Freddy' added Mr Hastings as he wagged his finger accusingly at the pug who was pushing into Andy's leg under the table, optimistic that Andy would slide a bit of his bun to him as he always did despite the disapproving look of Mr Hastings who was ever watching Freddy's ability to hoover up food and improve his comfortable girth.

Andy had pleaded with Mary, his mum, to get a pup when Mr Hastings had acquired Freddy as he said, 'For comfort,' when Mrs Hastings had gone to a, 'Higher place,' as he put it!

Andy's mum had said, 'No, with me working and you away at school all day it would not be fair on a pup.

Perhaps one day when I stop working we will talk about it again.'

When Andy's mum made up her mind, Andy knew better than to challenge her decision.

Andy had become accustomed to living in the two-bedroom flat on his own. He felt comfortable and safe there despite missing his Mum's presence, despite the care and attention to his everyday needs by Mrs Elsie Giles from flat eight next door who came in every day as arranged by his mother when she went into the Hospice. 'To keep you tidy until I get back, and no back chat to Elsie, young man, or I will hear about it!'

Andy felt it important to be able to manage for himself now he was very nearly sixteen and although he explained this to Mr Hastings over their cup of tea, 'this was only temporary,' as he delivered the papers, he knew deep down without ever admitting it out loud, that he would have to manage on his own in the future.

The Hospice ladies laid on a marvellous tea party on his sixteenth birthday and Andy's mum had her hair done and got up especially for the event.

Mr Hastings came into the party and brought Andy a Track Day Training Event in a Mini Cooper car at the Goodwood Race Track as his birthday present that thrilled and overwhelmed Andy.

Despite all the cheerfulness, there was an awful feeling of dread in the atmosphere perhaps made a little more painful because of his mum's happiness in seeing how grown up Andy was becoming.

Three weeks later after the funeral, Mr Hastings came over to Andy's flat to tell him that his Mum had made him the sole Trustee of the Will. Although Andy was now an adult in the eyes of the law he hoped that Andy would see him as his friend and guardian.

They hugged and Andy did not bother to hold back his tears of unhappiness tinged with his relief that someone he respected would be able to help and guide him as he faced up being on his own and looking for work.

At the top of his agenda that he shared with Mr Hastings was, 'Will I be able to stay in the flat?'

Mr Hastings assured him that he would as his mum had left sufficient funds to cover running costs, 'But as long,' said Mr Hastings, 'As you don't forget to turn off the lights and the music centre when you go to bed'; a favourite nag of his mother. 'And when you are eighteen I shall be passing the deeds over to you as you can own the property legally then.'

Andy's school academic work was never better than 'average' as his grades had suffered badly with his mother's illness. The school had recognised that his concentration was elsewhere and getting a job as soon as he was able seemed to be the best way forward, according to the sympathetic career advice teacher.

Andy explained his lack of any real idea as to what he might do when he next saw Mr Hastings after he left the Comprehensive School at the end of the term.

Mr Hastings cleared the kitchen table and produced a thick file from the chest of drawers.

'I have been doing some work on this project'. Mr Hastings liked 'projects' on which to work. 'Bearing in mind your interest in mechanical things and particularly cars, I have had a talk with an old friend of mine who is the Production Director at the Morgan Motor Company down the road.'

Mr Hastings continued whilst opening the file.

'He says if you are interested he will show you around the company and now I think perhaps if we play this right, he might offer you one of the apprenticeship places the Government are sponsoring to get you going on a job and then we could see how things stand at the end of a year. The pay's not much but with what your mum left, you could certainly manage. What do you think?'

Andy was bowled over with the whole idea as he loved motors and the traditional Morgan sport cars he had watched going to and fro from the company site had always fascinated him. The opportunity to look around was an offer that raised his spirits enormously.

Mr Hastings took on the management of the visit to Mr Hargreaves, the Personnel Manager, with his usual project efficiency, even down to insisting Andy purchase a new dark two-piece suit in the sale at Broadleys, the local men's clothing shop.

'Look, you stick out of your old suit everywhere, you must be three inches taller than when your mum bought it' was his comment, 'and by the way we can afford some new shoes, and here is my best red and blue tie. We're going to make sure we "score a goal"." A favourite comment of Mr Hastings when he wanted a successful conclusion!

Andy enjoyed Mr Hastings training on how to 'present ourselves in the best possible light' and quickly assimilated an interview vocabulary to cover his lack of academic success, without over emphasising his last two years of family difficulties.

At home over several evenings Andy studied a book from the library on the Morgan Company's beginnings and he became fascinated by the Morgan +8 and +4 model development, so he felt well briefed to talk with confidence about the Morgan cars to Mr Hargreaves the Personnel Manager at the arranged meeting.

Mr Hargreaves explained at the start of the meeting that Andy was one of ten young men looking for the single apprenticeship and he had the lowest academic performance.

Questions were asked at the meeting and Andy, full of enthusiasm for the traditional Morgan two seater sports, felt he did well, but when he talked about the company's remarkable success with their Jap engine three wheel Morgan racing in the 1920s and 1930s in detail, with specific information on drivers and car specifications, he thought Mr Hargreaves might have been a little impressed.

On the following Tuesday an offer for a full job position arrived by letter, not the regret letter for the apprenticeship he was expecting.

As they talked about the offer over their customary tea and sticky buns, Andy and his guardian Mr Hastings, both agreed how Andy's mum would have been so proud and delighted that everything had worked out for her 'independent young man'!

OUT OF TOWN VISITORS

The board for the Cancer Drop-in Centre was heavy and putting it at the bottom of the stairs where it could be seen by anyone coming into the cul-de-sac from the High Street was difficult enough thought Gertie to herself, without this rain.

Gertie made sure the brightly coloured tripod sign was properly angled to offer all the information and welcome necessary to any of those who might be seeking the counselling and friendly support of the Centre for themselvcs or those nearest and dearest to them, support to be found by climbing the stairs to the front door of the Victorian terraced house Drop-in Centre.

Gertie had just dumped the board slightly to the left in the gravel under the bay window, ignoring the rain dribbling off her hat on to her glasses, when she almost felt, rather than saw, a large black limousine, whose rear windows were darkened, creeping, almost silently, up the narrow cul-de-sac until it was opposite her and the Drop-in Centre steps.

The passenger side front window slid halfway down and a faceless voice from the interior said.

'Lady, where will we find Carlos's restaurant round here?'

Gertie recognised a South-East London voice when she heard it, particularly one that sounded as if it had been washed over grave.

Not to be put out by this ominous vehicle or the disembodied voice, Gertie said.

'If you wait a minute I will enquire in the Cancer Centre,' in the voice she usually used when she was displeased with one of her several grandchildren.

Gertie climbed up the stairs and into the warmth of the large living room, now comfortably converted into the Reception area of the Centre.

'Molly, Sarah, Diana, take a look through the window at that black limo in the road. They are asking where Carlos's restaurant is. Keep back so they don't see you. They are down here from the East End, I'm sure.' Puffed Gertie, rather out of breath from climbing the steps.

The ladies all peered round the huge artificial flower collection in the bay window, without disturbing the curtains.

'They have to be gangsters,' said Molly cheerfully, 'Look at the size of the limo. It shouldn't be in the cul-de-sac anyway.'

Being the senior member of the Cancer Clinic team, Molly assumed her usual role of 'I'm in charge' when anything unexpected happened.

'I know where that Italian restaurant is. It's back on the main road and I'm sure the back entrance is at the top of our cul-de-sac.' Molly said this as she put on her coat.

'Keep an eye on me, girls,' she said as she moved to the door and went down the stairs.

The 'girls' now crowded to the bay winder while Gertie stood 'guard' at the top of the stairs in front of the open door trying, as much as a slightly overweight middle-aged woman can, to look like a 'Minder': to be in authority.

Molly gathered her most formidable face and went to the side door of the still ticking over black limo. The window slid silently down to meet her.

'I understand you are looking for Carlos's restaurant?' she said, using her 'I'm in charge' voice.

'Mam,' was the only response before the door silently opened to evacuate a tall man in a double-breasted long black coat, dark suit trousers and highly polished Italian shoes. When he stood up fully, ignoring the rain, to what Molly thought must be six feet, she also took in his black hair immaculately cut and lacquered.

'If you could help us, Mam, my colleagues and I are here to meet an associate in the restaurant and we are not familiar with the territory. Also we are a little late,' the man replied in a very soft voice.

Molly was somewhat taken aback by the young man's politeness and charm. Even his smile with a flash of gold teeth seemed appropriate in the situation.

'Well, the front entrance is back on the High Street, turn left and thirty yards on your left. There is no parking however and the traffic wardens are very active in this area.' Molly said this in a rather conspiratorial manner, not being a fan of the rather over officious wardens.

The tall dark young man, who Molly was now certain was Mafia, said, 'I wonder, Mam, if it would be inconvenient to you and your clinic if we left our car here in your cul-de-sac for twenty minutes while we go and meet our colleague? We could pay you a parking fee if you would accept this.'

'Oh that would not be necessary,' said Molly, 'We do not own the cul-de-sac and all our support team give their time free as we are not a commercial enterprise. It would not be inconvenient to me, or my ladies, or those unfortunates who will be visiting us, if you leave your car here, but if you are unlucky and a warden comes round, he would certainly fine you – they always do.'

The young man flashed his gold again and said, 'I understand that, Mam, we will deal with that if it happens.' His double-breasted coat opened as he waved to his three colleagues to get out of the black limo, and Molly fancied she saw the shape of a gun butt strapped to the Italian's side.

His dark, swarthy and immaculately over-coated colleagues, each of whom had politely half bowed as they climbed out of the limo, left without saying a word they followed their leader down the cul-de-sac towards the High Street.

Molly felt breathless as she climbed the stairs to where Gertie was holding open the front door in a state of suppressed excitement.

'You were so brave, Moll, standing up to those gangsters. Come and have a cup of tea,' exclaimed Gertie.

The "girls" crowded around Molly's desk, each with a cup of tea, leaving the two or three patients to their own devices.

Gertie said, 'When I was looking down from the third floor when the two gangsters got out of the back, I saw there were several car number plates on the car floor.'

'That settles it for sure,' said Sarah, 'They must be stealing cars.'

'Well hang on,' said Diana, who was always the cautious one, 'They could be in the garage trade.'

There was a universal feeling round the table that something had to be done about the 'gangsters' parked outside the Centre.

Molly took charge.

‘Well OK, I will call the police and tell them we have a large limo parked illegally up the cul-de-sac. Sarah you have the best memory, slip out whilst they are away and get the number plate without writing anything down in case they come back to find you writing things down about them. Then I will report them to the police.’

The plan worked well as two elderly regular clients arrived, making a bit of a fuss about climbing the rather steep stairs, allowing Sarah to help them along, so she stood where it was convenient to read the limo’s rear number plate.

Armed with the detail, Molly retreated to the back office where she called the town’s police station.

The young lady who answered the call announced herself as PC Allen.

‘Yes, can I help you?

- is this call an emergency matter?

- do you require a police presence?

- do you require an ambulance?

- have you called about this matter on a previous occasion?

- we do record this call for service support reasons.’

PC Allen said all this without seeming to pause or take a breath.

Molly finally replied.

‘Well no, none of those things actually, I just wanted to report an illegal parking in Lady-Down cul-de-sac and I have the car number.’

‘I see,’ said PC Allen firmly.

‘I should transfer you to ‘traffic’ on Extension 9 but they are at tea break so I will take the details’. She said this with the sort of voice that indicated she normally only dealt with homicides and this matter was well below her rank and responsibility.

None the less, she intoned.

‘Do you know the owner of the vehicle?’

‘No,’ said Molly, ‘We only met when he arrived, so I don’t actually know if he is the owner’.

‘I see,’ said a clearly displeased PC Allen, ‘Car plate number?’

Hastily Molly gave the number and letters.

‘What time was the vehicle abandoned?’ was PC Allen’s next question.

‘Well I cannot be sure the car is abandoned, the man said he was coming back.’

Molly felt guilty giving this reply.

‘Please give your name, full address and a telephone number where our officers can contact you,’ concluded PC Allen.

By this point Molly felt she was the guilty party and sorry she had thought it necessary to report the gangsters' car.

She recounted the story to the ladies of her brush with police authority and they shared their concern but agreed in the end that they did what any right-minded citizen would have done. Anyway by this time the Centre was as full with those who needed advice and support from the Cancer Centre volunteers.

A week later a traffic officer in full regalia pushed the button at the top of the Centre stairs and asked to see Molly. He politely explained that the limousine plates had been from a stolen vehicle but they had been unable to spot the limousine on its return to London. Although they felt it likely the car was transporting a known East London gang, who were long established and well known in the East End.

The officer courteously thanked Molly and said,

'Not to worry as they would keep a watch for the car in their area but the gang rarely strayed out of their own territory.'

The ladies were excited but not surprised about the news and their brush with the gangster world and the Law.

A further week later the doorbell rang and an elderly, heavily accented lady asked to see the 'Mistress of the house.'

Molly showed the grey haired lady with a significant bun and beautiful pearl earrings and necklaces, to a seat in her office.

It turned out that this visitor was the wife of Carlos, the restauranteur, who had passed away the week before having suffered, as his wife explained, with a shaky heart.

'Too much good living,' as Mrs Carlos bluntly put it.

She then handed over a brown paper parcel.

'From the brothers,' she said.

'Presumably' thought Molly, 'Her recently met limo passengers.'

'The brothers want you to have this token of their appreciation of your assistance, to help the Centre along.'

With this said she placed the parcel in Molly's hands and departed without another word.

When Molly opened the brown paper parcel, neatly tied with string, in front of her ladies, they found to their amazement Five thousand pounds in twenty-pound notes, all in bank wrappers.

A sum which would cover the running costs of the Drop-In Centre for three months, and as she recovered from the shock Molly said, with considerable enthusiasm, 'Replace those dreadful old bay window curtains.'

There was a thoughtful silence before Diana, whose husband was a volunteer fireman said, to general approval.

'Normally I would suggest Molly should consider telling the police but thinking about their performance over the limousine, my vote is we should just accept this support and move on.'

THE MAINTENANCE MAN

Although the Hospice Receptionist must have seen how anxious he was she did not show it, getting him to sit in the comfortable reception area with a cup of tea whilst she called to the Personnel Department, where he heard her explain to someone that,

'A gentleman here in Reception would like to find out if there is a job vacancy in the Maintenance department?'

The receptionist did not elaborate by saying, as he had explained to her, he was recently retired and was looking for a part-time job.

A minute or so later a young lady in a white coat and a broad smile, advanced towards Jim, her hand extended.

'I understand you would like to join our Maintenance team?' she enquired.

Jim managed to evacuate his comfortable seat and stood to shake hands.

'Good morning, I'm Helen the Personnel Manager,' she said.

‘Jim Pearce,’ he replied, ‘Good morning, I was wondering if there was any opportunities for an experienced Maintenance man.’

Leading Jim upstairs to her small and somewhat cluttered office, made friendly by photos of a boy and girl on the beach with a dog and a man, who Jim supposed must be Helen’s partner as he had noticed her hands were free of any rings.

The tiny office was brightened by a beautiful purple orchid on the window ledge. Helen saw the orchid had caught Jim’s eye.

‘Beautiful isn’t it, everyone loves to see it. It was given to me a few days ago by a lonely lady who came to the Hospice for several weeks to visit her husband.’ She did not elaborate further.

Jim saw there was water in the saucer under the orchid pot.

‘They like to be quite dry,’ he said.

‘Oh, are you an expert? I really wasn’t sure how to look after the plant,’ Helen replied.

‘Not really,’ said Jim, ‘But I have several and although I am no gardener, I have learned they last longer out of direct sunlight and are happy with a weekly watering, and they don’t seem to prosper standing in water.’

‘Oh that’s so helpful,’ said Helen, tipping the surplus water into a plastic cup and moving the orchid to the corner of her bookshelf.

In the next half hour Jim found himself explaining things he had not been able to talk to anyone about in the three months since his work contract had expired, right on his sixty-fifth birthday, and despite the departmental lunch and Chairman's kind words highlighting a few events over his forty years in the Maintenance team, there was no offer of continued part-time employment that he had hoped might have been possible.

'It isn't the money,' as Jim explained to Helen, 'I have modest needs, particularly since my wife passed away. I just feel I still have something to offer but I have not found anyone willing to take on an ex-maintenance worker from a Crematorium! Something to do with the job environment I suppose,' said Jim to Helen sadly.

'No one wants to have you in the business after you have looked after the equipment to shift thousands of people's ashes!'

'Any way that's really why I'm here' Jim continued. 'I figured with all my experience of dealing with the mechanisms of people departing, perhaps I could find a way of moving up the ladder a little and do something useful for those still on this planet and I thought if I was allowed to work in the Maintenance team here at the Hospice I could contribute part time and to be honest, Helen, I have found the 'retirement' process rather lonely.'

Jim looked down at his large, rather calloused hands twisting on his lap.

Helen cleared her throat.

'Look Jim, we don't have a vacancy right now because the CEO has cut our budgets in several areas. I'm sure you know we live on gifts and donations and despite how generous people are and the local business community is, we do struggle to keep the seven-twenty-four service going to manage the thirty beds that are so important to support at least three thousand people each year in this community who need our services at the end of their lives.'

Helen sat back in her chair and then looking directly at Jim, continued.

'I have been thinking whilst we talked. I think you are exactly the sort of chap to fit into our team and if you were prepared to give us, say three days a week free of cost, for a couple of months, I am pretty sure with the new budgets in three months you would be in line for the vacancy we do need to fill, and you would also know if you are comfortable with the job and with the team of three who are stretched to keep things going for us today.'

Jim did not hesitate.

'Thank you, Helen, I would like to take up your suggestions. If you agree I can start on Monday and come in Wednesday and Friday.'

Ten minutes later Jim had signed the necessary papers and having thanked the receptionist, left the Hospice in a very cheerful mood, feeling his life had taken a definite turn for the better.

Three months later Jim knew as much about the water heating system, the electrics and power, and the complicated window security locking mechanisms in the Hospice building as anyone in the Maintenance team. He was also accepted by all and sundry as a helpful, kindly man, always ready to lend a hand whatever the task as he toured the site during his three days each week.

Jim quickly realised how to "fix" the rather decrepit heating boilers essential to keep the Hospice patients warm, and having taken the Instruction books for the thirty year old equipment home, he quickly found out that there was little that could be done for the system except "bodge" each fault to keep people warm, despite having found several system "shortcuts" to ensure the pumps and burners would keep going as winter approached.

As the weeks went by Jim found as he fixed and adjusted things, from light switches to curtain rails in the patients' rooms, he became comfortable in responding to those who were strong enough, or interested enough, to want a chat although he also became sensitive to when it was necessary to carry out his job in silence when the situation required it.

Jim also learnt from other members of the maintenance team as well as comments often made to him, as his popularity grew, by the nursing team of those rooms that had few or no family or friends visiting for one reason or another.

Having been through a period of loneliness himself, Jim was very sensitive to those who had no one to call on them in their last few days and he went out of his way to take a little longer over his task and to chat about this and that when the patient responded.

It was in pursuit of this extended Hospice role that Jim met Harold, a new patient at the end of his life, who had no family he knew of and had as he explained to Jim.

'Given my life to develop my garage business to the detriment of a family life and a lack of real friends and now here I am at sixty-five with terminal cancer and no one to call in and give me a chat.'

Jim soon found as he popped in to see Harold that in a way he and Harold had quite a lot in common and talking about mechanical things came easy to both of them, so much so that after a few days Jim asked Helen if he could visit Harold as a 'volunteer' after he finished work.

Helen was most enthusiastic.

'Of course, here is a "Volunteer" badge. I am sure Harold would appreciate your time and interest.'

On looking at the screen with his medical records, Helen went on to say, 'Unfortunately Harold really only has a few days left with us.'

Jim visited for an hour or two every day and shared his interest in the Hospice equipment with Harold, engineer to engineer!

Jim arrived to take on his Friday shift to hear the sad, if unexpected news that Harold had passed away peacefully in the night.

Jim felt really downcast and decided that he would like to respect their short, but friendly, relationship with Harold by going to his funeral and Helen gave him the arrangements the Hospice had made.

As a result, the following Wednesday Jim found himself back at his old place of work at the Crematorium. This time sitting in the back row of the almost empty Chapel as the undertakers slowly brought in the casket and placed it with their usual care and attention in front of the curtain, ready for Harold's last journey.

Helen and two of the Hospice nurses sat in the front row as the resident Crematorium Vicar said some appropriate words, no doubt thought Jim, given the background by Helen.

Before the hymn and the slow, and Jim noted, nicely smooth closing of the curtain as the coffin slid silently out of view, Jim was about to get up, collect his one and only trilby hat and leave, when the leader of the undertaker company came over and bending close to Jim said quietly.

'Hello, Jim, long time no see. I hope things are going well for you?'

And with this said he handed Jim an official looking buff envelope with "Attention of Jim Pearce" across the front.

Jim looked at the envelope with some interest. As the funeral party leader moved away he opened the letter and read with considerable surprise.

"Dear Jim, thank you for your time and support at the Hospice. I only wish we had met earlier as I am sure we would have become firm friends and in your open hearted way you made up for some of my thoughtless ways. You have now given me the opportunity to give something of value back, as long as you will help me."

The letter continued.

"My trustees have been instructed to authorise payment for a completely new hot water boiler and radiation system to be fully installed through the Hospice, whatever the cost, provided you will take the responsibility as the Project Manager and your decisions on the type of equipment and installation programme is final.

The CEO and Board of the Hospice will be receiving the instructions and the gift detail in the next few days. Please help me do this. I know you will do a good job. Thank you for all your support, your friend, Harold."

Jim sat in his old place of work and wept a little for a departed friend.

CHANGING CAREERS

The Help the Heroes Mobility Assessor left with a strong handshake and a confident smile as he said,

'Same time next week, Tim, and keep going with the exercises, you really are making good progress.'

Tim shut the flat door and limped back into his kitchen to put on the kettle for a cup of tea, conscious now that his prosthetic leg was causing his left stump discomfort after the hour's exercise.

Back in his living-come-bedroom, Tim sat on the small couch and considered his future as he had many times over the six months since the mine explosion had parted him from most of his left leg. He reflected he could live on his military disability pension, if he was careful. Somehow this thought gave him no pleasure.

Tim's twenty years of military training had left him with no real skills for Civilian Street now that any form of security, driving or training advisory roles were effectively barred and he no longer gave the newspapers or service literature ads any consideration.

Thinking of his situation once again Tim decided to be more organised and took out two blank sheets of paper and carefully wrote at the top of one “My Facts” and on the top of the other he wrote “My Emotions.”

The “Facts” sheet was quickly dealt with: 39 years of age, single, no skill for administrative work, disability pension, modest financial savings boosted by the sale of his much loved MG Sports car. His only known relative Uncle Morris, thanks in part Tim thought ruefully to a never-ending series of overseas postings and the loss of both his parents within three weeks of each other, Tim reminded himself painfully, whilst he was in Afghanistan.

Tim noted down he only had a month left in the Army flat provided as it was close enough to ‘hop’ to the Training and Rehabilitee Centre supported by the Help the Heroes charity.

Tim turned to the “Emotions” list and found putting down points much more difficult or, as he reflected, to be honest about.

Tim sucked the end of his biro pen and tried to sort his thoughts out.

“I have no career prospects,” he wrote. “I have no idea what I am going to do with the rest of my life,” and he nearly put down ‘as a cripple’ and decided that really was one step too far in feeling sorry for himself.

Next he wrote, “No prospects of a relationship.”

Tim had a refill cup of tea as he considered how Julie had extracted herself from their on-off relationship as soon as the extent of his injury had become clear. He had felt no anger on receiving the letter whilst lying on his back in the medical base, accepting her calmly explained decision based upon her needs to have a 'permanent' relationship and children before it was 'too late.'

Once again Tim felt the common sense in Julie's decision and the fact that whilst they had enjoyed many good times together, he really could not imagine settling down with Julie.

At the end of an hour's thought, Tim was left with two issues.

A need to commit himself to the Service Retraining Programme when he probably could qualify for a clerical job in an office somewhere, with a real prospect of the Help the Heroes charity finding him a place, and to find his Uncle Morris.

Tim decided on the latter course of action as the first target, a task which helped him avoid thinking about his life as a clerical misfit.

Finding Uncle Morris, his father's younger brother, turned out to be less difficult than he had thought, thanks to the laptop provided to him as part of the rehabilitation support programme.

Using the app "Trace Your Family," within an hour of following up the leads beginning with his grandfather's home and his and the family's community activities in Bembridge, Isle of Wight, Tim had located Cecil Gordon Morris in Bradford, Yorkshire, having disregarded several Morrises based upon his uncle's 1930 birth year and the unusual Gordon middle name.

A helpful telephone operator offered to put Tim through to a number in the Heaton district of Bradford and his call was promptly answered by a male voice, sounding very much like Tim's father, bringing back some painful memories.

The call was warm and open and CG, as he liked to be known, was most solicitous when he discovered his nephew had been seriously damaged in Afghanistan.

Tim took all the blame for not finding him earlier and informing him of events after his brother's death.

In the same spirit CG said he had been surprised that Tim had not got back for the funerals but understood the difficulties of leaving his troop in intense combat conditions going on at the time in Afghanistan.

CG pressed Tim to agree to visit him in Yorkshire and Tim was delighted to respond positively and a date was agreed.

Tim came off the phone in a far happier frame of mind than he had before trying to trace his uncle.

A week later Tim limped up to the ticket barrier in the Victorian splendour of Bradford Central Railway Station, to find a replica of his father waiting to greet him with a warm hug and a beaming smile.

Back in the comfortable semi-detached house with its small but immaculate garden Tim found his bedroom comfortably appointed with everything he might need for his stay and the suggestion that after freshening up they might retire to the local hostelry for supper.

CG made it clear that his cooking was 'not up to much' as ever since Tim's Aunt Rosie had passed away, CG had taken to eating out once during the day. This was usually in the evening as his job on the Checkout counter of the largest Garden Centre on the outskirts of the city, kept him happily busy for six days a week.

The atmosphere between Tim and CG already convivial was warmed up in the pub with the help of a couple of large whiskies and Tim was able to share his concerns for his future and his lack of a career with his Uncle.

CG was immediately practical and suggested he would take Tim into the Garden Centre the next day where Mr Cripps, the Manager, 'who is a friendly soul and a man of considerable experience and might well have some ideas for Tim to consider.'

As it turned out the next day Mr Cripps went out of his way to be helpful after CG had explained his nephew's background and the reason for his visit.

Seated comfortably in Mr Cripps's large office surrounded by the paraphernalia of a busy Garden Centre including, as Mr Cripps explained, a range of exotic pot plants from Asia that Mr Cripps, now Harry, explained he had to make some decisions about taking on as a new line for the Centre.

The problem Harry explained to Tim was that his customers are constantly looking for more and more exotic plants, both indoors and outdoors, encouraged by TV gardening programmes and media cover promoting the latest and most unusual shrubs, trees and flowers.

'Now, Tim,' said Harry, 'If you could take an interest and specialise in something that could be marketed through a Garden Centre, you might have a way of developing a career that would provide you with the independence you are clearly looking for. I have told the management team you are a friend of the owners and you will be walking around all the departments. OK hopping,' as Tim interjected and both laughed.

Harry continued, 'Over the next couple of days see if you can find something which interests you that might help us at the Garden Centre as well. CG has filled us in with details of your determination to find yourself a new career. He was so pleased to get together as a family because as you know he has been very lonely since he lost Rosie. Now just treat the place like your own and we will chat whenever you have any, and I do mean any, ideas.'

The next few days were an enjoyable tonic for Tim moving around the various departments offering books, clothes, food as well as plants and flowers at different levels in the Centre. Working his way indoors and outdoors where the ground levels between the plant and shrub sections was anything but regular, gave Tim a great deal of balance practice until on his third day visit he had enough confidence to leave his walking stick in the General Office and make his way about reliant upon his prosthetic leg.

When he returned at tea break he was embarrassed and pleased to receive a standing applause from the staff.

Using his military service experience to observe and note his immediate environment, Tim built up a body of information that he thought might lead to activity for him, and over the several discussions with CG during their convivial evenings the area most suited to his military background, leaving aside his 'emotional' interests that Tim felt had been blown out of him by the roadside mine.

During their discussions and as they became more familiar with each other, Tim had agreed to CG's suggestion that he find an apartment in Bradford, delighted that his Uncle wanted to extend the family friendship.

The ground floor flat CG found for him in the Heaton district of the city, on the edge of the Ilkley Moors, was far more spacious and well-appointed than anything he could have afforded in the South and within a few days his small bundle of personal effects arrived and he was comfortably installed.

The flat also had the advantage of a commodious garage which Tim decided he could conveniently use as an office as it was well insulated and had a window over the garden.

CG was an enthusiastic helper and within no time an old desk had been found and was installed with shelving and a telephone extension from the flat.

Tim had not had much time to consider what 'hardware' material he might focus upon but he had noted in his list that whilst the Garden Centre had a small range of bonsai trees for sale, there was no support equipment, fertilizer or pots, nor even books giving advice to those interested, and Tim decided this should be his first target.

Harry Cripps was enthusiastic in his support when Tim cautiously suggested he would like to research and find suppliers who would have a range of ancillary products that might encourage increased sales in bonsai trees.

Tim left Harry's office feeling he had a real project to get his teeth into for the first time since the day he took out his last patrol in Afghanistan.

Sitting in his new 'office,' Tim found that whilst there were a number of retailers with a range of bonsai trees and related products, they were all Asian-based and not helpful when he tried to enquire about prices and distribution discounts.

The more time he spent on the phone and his laptop, the more he realised he needed more background about the bonsai trees themselves and something of the bonsai culture.

A cup of tea and a discussion with Gerald, whose supervisory responsibilities covered ‘small sections’ that encompassed everything from a range of items including, floral, toilet accessories, garden seats and bonsai trees.

Gerald said he had several times phoned up a local private bonsai enthusiast who had been extremely helpful in giving technical information about the trees when a customer had a query.

Armed with a Mr Peter Chinn’s telephone number, Tim prepared what he hoped was a list of questions that might help him understand the bonsai culture.

Within minutes of explaining to Mr Chinn that he was working with the Garden Centre and doing some research into bonsai trees, he found himself invited to Mr Chinn’s house on the outskirts of the city.

Arriving by taxi down a quiet lane which led upwards on to the Yorkshire Moors, Tim found himself enthusiastically welcomed by a small and wizened Hong Kong Chinese gentleman whose enthusiasm to talk about bonsais knew no bounds.

Peter Chinn had prepared a tray offering Mint tea and wafer like biscuits as he courteously enquired about Tim’s reasons for his interest in bonsai.

Tim found himself explaining his loss of professional direction and his difficulties of coming to terms with his disability as he tried to find a new meaning and direction in his life.

To his surprise Tim found himself openly sharing emotional feelings he had not brought to the surface as Peter Chinn gently probed his reasons for visiting.

After their tea Peter took Tim through the back of immaculate house, having explained his wife was making her annual pilgrimage to see relatives in Hong Kong, and thence into a sizeable back plot running up to a steep rise of open Moorland.

The space was filled with timber buildings, some slatted, some glazed, all with shelving upon which were hundreds of bonsais of every size and shape.

Peter stopped by a twisted tree no more than 18 inches high, the knarred and bleached wood somehow complementing the healthy green pine leaves and the draped down umbrella shape. The tree was in a pine green and gold ceramic pot, standing on three legs each flattened outwards on the bench.

'This tree is one of my best and is one hundred and eighty years old,' said Peter, 'I acquired this Japanese white pine more than thirty years ago. It's quite famous now, having taken several awards over the years as a classic tree.'

Peter led on, stopping to introduce several of his favourite trees, as he continued to explain his passion for the trees.

'This is a Maple in the class we call "Shohin" because it's still under twelve inches high but it is growing at the same rate as its wild brother so we have to prune the roots every year and you see how this branch is wired to give the tree the shape I am looking for. I have been working on this beautiful tree for ten years and expect to do so for another ten before I might show it in a bonsai exhibition.'

Tim was fascinated as Peter showed him several more of his favourite trees and when he invited Tim to join his weekly bonsai meeting, Tim was delighted to accept the opportunity.

Over the next few weeks Tim entered a completely new world based upon the two thousand year old Buddhist skills of developing and presenting trees in miniature over tens, and sometimes, hundreds of years.

Tim's military disciplines played a part as he documented, checked and listed trees most suited to bonsai, identifying the importance of getting the bowl to complement the tree with the vision of the final shape well in mind.

Tools and techniques for wiring branches into shape and the essential annual root pruning all became part of his daily study and research. As did his collection of English tree seedlings, elm, juniper, pine and beach, where as Peter put it,

'You can anticipate propagate leaf size and remember any fruit or flowers will grow to the same size as the wild tree. It can be a nice feature of your bonsai but you will need to bear it in mind as you shape your tree.'

The Garden Centre boss was delighted to have Tim's new expertise available for his customers and perhaps more emotionally rewarding to Tim was when he put together a "Practical Guide into Bonsai Tree Growing" and sent it down to the Disabled Soldiers' Recovery Centre as being of possible interest, he was rewarded by the CO phoning to ask if he could do a monthly article in the Rehabilitation Journal circulated to all damaged Service personnel and Tim put down the phone realising he had put aside one of his emotional anxieties.

The next day in the Garden Centre he recounted the exciting news to Harry, who said:

'Excellent news which fits right into my plans as thanks to your commitment and determination we have had a great deal more interest in the bonsai section, and so I hope you will take on a supervisory role for us.'

As Tim nodded and smiled his pleasure, Harry said:

'That's just as well because I have already organised your outfit,' and with this he passed Tim a box with a light green set of trousers and a tank top, resplendent with Supervisor embroidered on the sleeve in yellow and Tim's name on the breast pocket.

Harry said, with considerable emotion, 'Well, you're back in uniform now, soldier,' as he gripped Tim's hand.